The Blinks

'Self-Esteem'

by Andrea Chatten

Illustrations by Rachel Pesterfield

To Andrea,

Lots of love

Andrea Chatter

o xx

First published in 2015 by

The Solopreneur Publishing Company Ltd

Cedars Business Centre, Barnsley Road, Hemsworth, West Yorkshire WF9 4PU

www.thesolopreneur.co.uk

ISBN 978-0-9934527-0-3

Printed in the U.K.

For further copies, and other titles in the series, please go to - www.oodlebooks.com. Also available on Amazon and Kindle.

Contents

Contents

Dedication

This book is dedicated to Granny Gran for her 96th year and who is one of the most inspirational women I know.

Chapter 1

The twins

I would like to introduce you to Bladen and Tim.

You are going to get to know Timeo (otherwise known as Tim) and Bladen very well throughout this story, but it would be good for you to know some key facts. First, they are twins. Obviously not identical, but many similarities nevertheless!

Here are some of the things that make Bladen and Tim alike:

1. They both have dark brown hair.

2. They are eleven years old.

3. They are half Irish and half Jamaican.

4. They are clever but don't realise it.

5. Neither of them likes ice-cream.

6. They are not very popular.

7. They support Sheffoold City Football Club.

8. To them tomato sauce is repulsive.

9. They have little self-confidence.

10. They love watching TV.

11. When they go to sleep, they curl up in a ball.

12. They love dogs.

13. They don't like themselves very much.

However, they also have many differences just as most brothers and sisters do. These are some of the things that make them very different:

1. Tim is a boy. Bladen is a girl.

2. Bladen is taller than Tim.

3. Tim plays the guitar. Bladen plays nothing.

4. Tim keeps his feelings in, whereas Bladen shouts about them.

5. Tim loves Braincraft on the computer. Bladen hates computer games.

6. Bladen loves skateboarding. Tim has no sense of balance.

7. Tim is brilliant at magic tricks. Bladen cannot keep a secret.

8. Bladen cries a lot. Tim tries to ignore his feelings.

9. Bladen has long hair. Tim has short hair.

10. Tim tends to punch in a fight. Bladen kicks.

As you can see from many of the things on their lists, Bladen and Tim are not living the dream!

Now and then, the things they have in common create a lovely moment. Once, they made up a pop song that Tim played on the guitar and Bladen sang the words to. This kept them entertained for hours. Sadly, it all went wrong when they performed it to the family one Sunday afternoon. Both thought that the other was getting more attention because they were a better performer!

This argument came up a lot of the time.

The problem occurred because neither of them liked themselves very much and so were needy of things that proved they might be okay. They both wanted things in life that made them feel good. Sometimes that was the latest computer game or the trendiest shoes. Now and then, their parents bought them these things, in the hope that Bladen and Tim might become happier children and all would be fixed, like waving the magic wand in Tim's box of tricks!

The other part of this complicated problem was that both Bladen and Tim spent way too much time looking at how other people behaved and not enough time realising the many wonderful qualities that they had right there inside themselves. Neither of them helped each other out in this area either.

Tim was the first to remind Bladen of all her bad points, and vice versa!

An example of this happened one

Sunday morning when both children were doing their homework and Mum was preparing vegetables for the Sunday roast later that evening.

"Mum, how do you work out the area of a triangle again?" asked Tim scrunching up his face in confusion.

"Don't you even know that? That is so easy. We only did that last week," gloated Bladen.

"Shut up, Bladen, you don't know everything," snapped Tim.

"Hey you two, that's enough. Bladen, get on with what you're doing and stop interfering. Right Tim, you should know this as I'm sure we did this last weekend too," echoed Mrs O'Brien.

"Ha ha even Mum thinks you're stupid," sniggered Bladen.

Tim dropped his head in disappointment.

"Bladen, that's enough! Go and do your homework somewhere else and stop being so nasty," shouted Mum.

Bladen looked wounded and ran off to her bedroom feeling very upset that Mum had just called her nasty.

"Bladen," shouted Mum. But she had gone.

"Oh dear! Why do we have this every time? You are both as bad as each other. You both say hurtful things to each other but can't take it when the other one says something hurtful back. Neither of you are happy because of it, so what is the point?" asked Mum.

"It's because she's horrible, Mum. I hate her," whimpered Tim.

"That's a bit harsh. Hate is a strong word, even if she can be nasty sometimes. Right, let's forget about all of this and get on with the area of a triangle. It is half length of the base times the height. Look."

Mum then drew several triangles with different measurements and got Tim to work them out while she continued at the sink with the vegetables.

What neither of them realised was that Bladen had been sitting on the stairs the whole time and had heard Tim say he hated her, and Mum say she was nasty. She started to cry. Why hadn't Mum come to see if she was okay? This must mean they both hated her. Well, of course they would, because even Bladen hated herself.

In the kitchen, Tim was still doing his homework and had come across another maths question that he wasn't sure about. He couldn't ask Mum again, as she already thought he was stupid for not knowing the triangle question. What was he going to do? He would just have to get that one wrong. And the next one and the next one. Tim hated homework.

Bladen had gone to her bedroom and was still crying on her bed, hating Tim because Mum obviously loved him more, and hating herself for being such a horrible person. As she wept, she slowly drifted into sleep.

As she dreamed, Bladen visited all the situations that made her feel let down or a failure. She recalled the time she dropped the milk bottle out of the fridge and her Dad really shouted at her for being so careless and clumsy. She then thought about the times when she had got a question wrong in school and everybody laughed at her, and once when she was left behind at the park after a friend's birthday party because Mum was running late. Finally, she remembered the time that she spent hours tidying her room without being asked, and no-one noticed.

She then went to a place she wished that she could forget. The worst place ever. This was when she was six years old and made up a story that she had got a horse for her birthday. All the children in the class thought it was brilliant and exciting.

For a while she felt popular, interesting and proud. She continued with the story for weeks and was beginning to believe it herself.

Misty was a grey pony, with a black mane. He was in a stable not too far away. She went riding on him every weekend and was going to learn to do some jumps. At school, Bladen and her friends even played horses. They would canter around the playground and playing field, riding imaginary ponies that every now and then would rear up and take a lot of strength to rein them back in.

Then the fantasy balloon popped! With a huge boom!!!!

One warm Saturday morning while Bladen was lolling around watching TV, there was a knock on the door. It was Evie Mae, one of her school friends, all dressed up in a riding hat, boots and those posh riding trousers with padding around the bottom. She was with her mum.

Evie Mae wasn't just any school friend, she was becoming Bladen's best ever friend since they had started the pony club. No-one enjoyed riding imaginary horses more than Evie Mae and from this new love, a special friendship was forming.

"Look what my cousin has just given me," squealed Evie Mae holding her hands out in a way that made it seem that she had arrived there by magic.

"Wow, you look amazing. Do you want to play horses?" asked Bladen, not realising what was just about to happen.

"Yes, but not pretend, I thought I could come with you today when you go to ride Misty. We can play real horses," said Evie Mae with more excitement than Bladen had ever seen.

"I just thought I had better check that this was okay with your mum first, Bladen, as Evie Mae has been telling me all about your new pony and how you ride him every weekend. Is your mum in?"

asked Mrs Hocken.

Bladen did not know what to say. She was just about to pretend that her mum was ill when Mrs O'Brien came down the stairs.

"Hello, Evie Mae. You look very smart. Are you off to a riding event?" asked Mum smiling at Mrs Hocken, who she had spoken to once or twice in the playground.

"Well, she is hoping that she can come with you today. I know we have just dropped it on you, but Evie Mae has been so excited since Bladen got her horse and now that my niece has given her all the riding gear, I couldn't hold her back!" explained Mrs Hocken.

Mum looked at Bladen and Bladen looked up at Mum.

"Bladen, please go to your room and we will talk about this later," said Mum in a stern voice.

As Bladen walked nervously up the

stairs, she heard her mum explaining that there was no horse. By way of an apology, Mum invited Evie Mae to stay and play horses, but it would definitely not be on a real one.

Evie Mae's sobbing could be heard from far and wide. Bladen got a serious telling off from Mum, who had been very embarrassed by her lies.

Yet being shouted at by Mum was the easiest part of the whole affair. Worse than any telling off was the fact that she lost her best ever friend. Everyone in school knew about it. All her classmates thought that she was a liar. But worst of all, they all still played horses - her game, and she was not allowed to join in. This dream was more of a nightmare.

While Bladen was sleeping, Mum popped in to see if she was okay, but left her be when she saw that her little girl was happily snoozing.

Bladen eventually woke up feeling worse

than she did before she went to sleep. She then felt even sadder when she realised that no-one had even come and checked she was okay. This is how Bladen felt most of the time, because her self-esteem (self-love) was so low. At that moment, she felt like the loneliest person in the whole world, and this feeling was becoming her only friend.

Chapter 2

A secret mission!

As Bladen lay on her bed, her thoughts were being driven by all the reasons why she was an unlovable person. All the things that people had said to her in the past were scribbled inside her brain like graffiti, as constant reminders. She let her mind's eye read some of the thoughts that she had about herself:

- You are stupid
- No-one likes you
- You are a nasty person
- You have no friends
- Mum likes Tim more than you
- You are and always will be a liar

This was a tough read. The more Bladen read it, the sadder and emptier she felt. She never wanted to go downstairs again. How could she face Mum and Tim knowing how they felt about her?

Just then, the telephone rang. Mum quickly headed from the kitchen into the living room and removed the phone from its holder. "Hello. Oh hi, Reo, how are you getting on with the water leak?"

Reo was Bladen and Tim's dad. He worked at a posh hotel on the outskirts of town, and it was his job to manage the building and any problems that might happen. Sadly that morning, he had been called out as there was a dripping toilet in one of the bedrooms. It wasn't just any bedroom. It was the Bridal Suite of the couple who were about to be married later that day!

Dad dreaded being called out to work at the weekend, as did Mum. From the conversation, Bladen could tell that the leak hadn't been as straightforward as Dad had wanted, but it sounded like he would be home quite soon. She then heard Mum tell Dad all about what had happened earlier.

"Honestly, like we want to spend our weekend with these two battling. I have had enough of this. Bladen was horrible to Tim earlier, any excuse to have a go. She can be so unkind sometimes."

At this point, Dad must have been replying, as Mum went quiet. Bladen was sure that he would be agreeing with Mum about what a horrible girl she was. Now she had Dad to face as well.

"Okay, love. We will see you later. Think about where we could go for tea tonight. Bye." Mum slipped the phone back into its holding stand and went back into the kitchen.

So Mum and Dad were going to go out for tea later because they couldn't bear to be around her and Tim anymore, thought Bladen. That would mean that they would need to go to Grandma and Grandad's, who would then also know about how mean she had been. Bladen thought she might as well just get an article written up in the local Gazette with a heading saying: 'Bladen O'Brien - the nastiest girl in the whole world!'

As Bladen lay there, she realised that

she was now becoming quite desperate for the toilet. Yet she did not want to leave the safety of her bedroom. What if they heard her moving from downstairs? They would be straight up to have another go at her. What if she bumped into one of them as she was leaving her bedroom? She would have to talk or, worse still, ignore them to keep up her 'horrible girl' act.

Oh no, what was she going to do? This was not a choice anymore, action was needed quickly, very quickly! She decided to tip-toe across her room while doing her best to avoid creaky floorboards. She succeeded without a sound. Stage one of her mission complete.

Stage two would be trickier. This involved squeezing out through the door (without opening it too much due to annoying squeaky hinges) and getting across the landing and into the bathroom with a now very full bladder!

Bladen put all of her senses on alert.

She couldn't see anyone out there. She could just about hear voices from the kitchen, suggesting that she was safe to make a very light-footed run for it.

Yes! She did it! As she landed inside the bathroom, she gently shut the door, pleased that her negative mood could be kept private without anybody needing to break it. Bladen was good at holding onto a negative mood and today she felt more justified than ever before.

While she was washing her hands (turning the taps on as slowly as possible in order to continue with the secrecy of her movements), she looked in the mirror at her face. Her eyes looked red from crying. Her lips were swollen. Not only was she horrible inside, but she was also very obviously horrible outside too. Another scribble was added to the wall of negativity in her brain – you are ugly.

Bladen felt as fed up as fed up could feel.

As she left the bathroom, she flushed the chain without thinking. Bladen would never normally flush after washing her hands; toilet hygiene was important to her. In fact, due to the situation, this time she wasn't going to flush at all. Years of training had caught her out though, and she just did it out of toilet habit. "Oh no," she thought, believing her cover might be blown.

She decided that the only thing to do was to go for it. She opened the door and headed straight back into her room, shutting the door behind her. As she rested backwards onto it with a sigh of relief, she felt safe again.

Seconds later there was a knock on the door. Bladen slid down, sitting herself upright and rigid in order to barricade herself in.

"Bladen, are you going to come down now so that we can put things right with you and Tim?" asked Mum.

Bladen stayed silent.

"Come on, we don't need this to go on all day. You do need to say sorry for what you said to Tim. That wasn't very nice."

Bladen couldn't believe what Mum was saying. What about all the hurtful things Mum had said to Bladen about her being nasty and horrible? This made her feel upset.

Then Bladen started to feel angry.

"Go away!" shouted Bladen. "You always stick up for Tim. You don't even like me because I am nasty and horrible, aren't I?"

"Oh, Bladen. Here we go again. If you don't want people to think that you are any of those things, then don't do nasty and horrible things. I will be downstairs when you are ready to talk about this properly," explained Mum, heading downstairs.

Bladen felt even more upset. Why hadn't Mum tried harder to make her feel better? Why couldn't Mum see that she was hurting behind that door? Bladen slumped putting her head in her hands. How could she turn all of this around? She was out of her depth.

Then Bladen felt something slide under the door. A folded piece of paper poked her bottom. Was this a message from Mum apologising for what she had said earlier and that Bladen wasn't a horrible and nasty girl after all?

She opened up the note. Inside it read:

Ha ha, you got done!

No-one likes you. You are mean.

Why don't you just stay in your room forever?

From Tim (your happy brother)

Bladen was furious. She opened the door just in time to see Tim disappear across the landing into his room and slam the door quickly. Bladen followed.

"I hate you. You are the worst brother in the world. Just you wait until you come out. You will wish you never did," shouted Bladen banging loudly on the door.

"Mum, Mum, she is going to hurt me," shouted Tim wimpily from inside his bedroom.

Mum rushed upstairs and moved Bladen away from the door.

"In your room, Bladen, now! Do us all a favour today and just stay there for a while. If you lay one finger on Tim, then you will have no screens for a week and that means iPads and computers. Do you hear me?" shouted Mum.

Bladen barged past Mum. Tim would love this even more. She would have shown Mum the note, but she couldn't see the point. Mum had made it very clear whose side she was on. She went back to her room and scrunched up the note, throwing it in the bin.

For a minute, she wished that she could scrunch up Tim and throw him in the bin too.

Bladen slumped down on the bed and wished that someone, anyone, could be on her side just for once. Why didn't anyone stick up for her?

From outside, perched on Bladen's bedroom windowsill, someone had been watching the events of the afternoon very closely. Could this person be *the someone* that Bladen wished for? Could *they* be the answer to Bladen changing these feelings around for the better?

Only time and sugar dough will tell.

Chapter 3

Blink business

It was quickly approaching midnight in Sheffoold; a very busy time for the Blinks. Across the darkened sky, hundreds of excited characters were heading towards Rosie's Bakery, ready for a very special meeting.

Blink 28770 Larry Love-Who-You-Are also had an extra spring in his step this evening as he felt that he had found the perfect project for him to become part of. However, he did have many questions to ask the wise ones, as this case was not like one he had ever worked on before.

As Larry Love-Who-You-Are arrived at the bakery, the gentle hum of Blink energy could be sensed through the cool midnight air. He was just in time, so found a place in front of the bread shelf where Chief Blink was getting ready to address the crowd.

"Good evening Blinks," began Chief Blink. "Please join me in celebrating all the hard work we have done over the last 24 hours. Hurray for goodwill and kind hearts!"

A cheer erupted from the bakery. Larry Love-Who-You-Are beamed with happiness along with his fellow workmates.

"I am feeling lots of excitement in the room tonight. This usually means that many of you are feeling ready to begin new projects. I feel it might be busy on the chocolate éclair tray so I will head there myself later to see how things are going. Okay Blinks, make your way to where you need to be. Have fun," said Chief Blink. The room buzzed with movement.

Larry Love-Who-You-Are tiptoed to the chocolate éclair trays where he had spent the last couple of weeks. Although he would never complain, he was desperate to move to stage two, which was actually his favourite part. He was hopeful that tonight might be the chance for that to change. As the Blinks scattered, it was obvious that there were many similarities between them all, such as their sequence numbers which show how long they have been around, shades of purple showing different forms of wisdom and a deep drive to help any child who is not as happy as they could be. However, each Blink is as individual as you and me.

Blinks can be one shade or many colours. They can be smart or casual, old or young. One place that they will always be though is inside a bakery, in the city where they live, by midnight. This is where all the Blinks have their magic renewed. It is also when the Blinks experience the five phases of Blinkery!

Stage 1...*On the lookout!* This stage is when the Blinks are looking out for kids who are struggling with life issues. The

Blinks are either in the research stage, trying to find a deserving child project, or are ready with a young person who they feel might be ready.

The chocolate éclair trays in the main display cabinet are where all Stage 1 Blinks meet. This is where new children are introduced and exciting new projects will begin.

If a Blink is still searching for the right child and situation, then the Blinks work together to create the sugar dough buffet. This involves hunting and gathering any stray crumbs or sugary delights that might be left over in the bakery that evening.

This sweet feast is enjoyed by all the Blinks at the end of the meeting. This is a delicious way of giving them the energy that they need for their next day of hard work, while also enjoying each other's company.

Stage 2...*A good start.* This involves the Blinks who are working with a child and everything is going as planned. These Blinks learn from each other's wisdom and use it to decide what they can do next.

Stage 2 happens on the vanilla slice board, also in the main display cabinet, but the corner furthest from the bakery's entrance. This is most often the quietest stage of Blinkery but also one of the most positive, as it is all about celebrating the good.

Stage 3...*Help!* This is the busiest stage, as most projects present challenges that need to be discussed. On the large wooden bread shelves that cover the whole back wall of the bakery, the Blinks get down to some serious life learning.

The Wise Ones are always on hand here to share past stories of the Blinks' history so that lessons can be learned. The Blinks know that listening at this stage is more important than talking!

Stage 4...*Eye spy.* When a project has finished, and the child has succeeded to

move things forward to a better place, the
Blinks end up here, on the fairy cake trays
that sit in the window, under large white
sheets of kitchen paper!

All Blinks would agree that this is one of
the best stages. At this stage, the Blinks
start to feel satisfied and proud but not
until they are 100% happy that all is
good, do they start looking for the next
child. This means that the real feelings of
satisfaction only begin after the monitoring
phase has happened. The Blinks see this
as a time to be on hand just in case things
go a little wrong, as many new changes
can. The Blinks have two important rules
at this stage:

1. Each child must tell at least
   one trustworthy person about
   the difficulties they have been
   feeling and what they have been
   doing now to make things better.
   The Blinks suggest this as it is
   crucial that all children know
   that they have someone they

can talk to. (Also, by sharing our problems, we connect with others so that they can support us when we need it most.)

This rule also means that the Blinks feel content that the child is no longer alone and so they can move more happily on to the next stage. When each Blink feels sure that each child is championed by someone else, the circle of Blink magic is complete.

2. This rule is probably the most important. Children must never mention the Blinks' help. Those who have very quickly regretted it, as the Blinks' input stopped from that very moment when Blink magic was spoken about. The Blinks' magic can, you see, twinkle forever in children's hearts if it remains pure and unspoilt.

Stage 5…*Whey hey!* When the Blinks
have a sense of pleasure that the child
has changed their negative situation into
a better one, then a period of celebration
can begin. For seven whole days after
the project has finished, beginning
at midnight the following day, much
enjoyment begins.

At this time the Blinks 'top up' every
good value in their souls. This is needed
to continue the Blinks' success, especially
after handing over their hearts and brains
to whoever they have just been working
with. The Blinks can do whatever they feel
will make this stage as fabulous as it can
be. Some of the Blinks meet up with other
Blinks, some lay back and reflect in the
satisfaction of a job well done. Whatever
they do, they do it because it makes them
feel happy and refreshed, ready for their
next exciting journey.

Each of the Blinks knows this system of
Blinkery instinctively and so Larry Love-
Who-You-Are wasted no time in getting

to where he needed to be. He was even more excited tonight, now that there was a possibility for him to discuss his findings with Chief Blink!

As Larry Love-Who-You-Are approached the chocolate éclair trays, he was considering all the evidence that made the O'Briens' an excellent next project to work on. He couldn't help but think about the factors that made this family not suitable, the biggest one being could he successfully work with twins!

The Stage 1 Blinks were enthusiastically squeezing into a circle, which is the way things usually begin. Larry Love-Who-You-Are nudged in between his two very good friends Blink 24370 Travis Train-Your Brain and Blink 10861 Sarah Success.

"Hi, you two. What has been good about your day today?" asked Larry Love-Who-You-Are cheerfully.

"Hey, Larry Love-Who-You-Are. Nice to see you. Well, lots of lovely things actually but by looking at the smile on your face, nothing quite as exciting as yours!" replied Sarah Success. "Have you found a new project?"

Just as Larry Love-Who-You-Are was about to answer, Chief Blink began. "Wow, my wonderful Blinks, your energy is electric tonight and that makes me happy that we are working well and supporting the valued children of Sheffoold. I understand that there are several new cases to be discussed this evening so if we could break into small groups and the Wise Ones and I will move around to talk with you about the children you have selected."

Small groups formed around the perimeter of the tray. Larry Love-Who-You-Are tried to judge which group would be more likely to get the chance to work with Chief Blink. Her role was almost royal within the Blinks' network. In the end, he decided that the chance of talking with her was completely random, so he went with a group that felt good enough and sat down.

Throughout the night, Larry Love-Who-You-Are heard many needy stories about kids from across the city who were desperate for the Blinks' help. Of all the people he told about his case, not even any of the Wise Ones had much experience of working with twins. No-one gave him a definite 'yes', which began to worry him slightly. Before he knew it, the meeting had come to an end and the sugar dough buffet was about to begin.

Larry Love-Who-You-Are wasn't sure what to do. He believed in Bladen and Tim. He had all the signs that this was a worthy project, the excited feeling in his tummy being the most important. As he was pondering his dilemma, Chief Blink came and stood beside him.

"I hear that you have found a double project, Larry Love-Who-You-Are? Twins are not an easy challenge," whispered Chief Blink.

"Yes I agree, Chief Blink. But all the facts about it make me feel that this case is right; I am feeling it deep inside me where our instincts are stored," answered Larry Love-Who-You-Are, feeling amazingly calm.

"I had a twins' case a long, long time ago and it was tough. From that case, we decided that one Blink to one child worked much better. I feel your passion and with the right support, I think we could give it a try," said Chief Blink. "If it is okay with you, Larry Love-Who-You-Are, I would like to be your Wise One throughout this project, if and when you need it."

Larry Love-Who-You-Are beamed. Not only did he now have the green light to work with Bladen and Tim, but he was also going to have the guidance of Chief Blink. "Yipppeeee," he squealed and fizzed off towards the sugar buffet.

"Wait for me," shouted Chief Blink, thrilled to see such joy from one of the Blinks.

Chapter 4

Thought bubbles

The next morning at exactly 7.04am, Bladen and Tim each woke from a very restless night's sleep. Neither knew that the other was awake, but sometimes the twin bond did strange things and today, this was one of those days. Both knew that they had exactly 26 minutes before Mum would be in to wake them up. As they lay there in their individual rooms, on their individual beds, they were having anything but individual thoughts.

Although both of them were more than aware that they had been unkind to the other yesterday, neither of them found it easy to admit mistakes. This usually caused them to become stuck in a cycle of negative thoughts. Tim's cycle included:

- Nobody likes me, not even my own sister

- I can't do anything right, I am so stupid

- I don't like my life

- I am a bad person

- I am not good at maths, or anything else

- I always get it wrong

- I hate feeling like this

Bladen's cycle looked like this:

- Tim hates me, everyone hates me

- I am a nasty person

- I am mean

- I do not deserve love

- I am rubbish at everything

- My life is pointless

- I hate feeling like this

As these thoughts floated from each of their minds, a huge thought bubble was being formed around them that neither of them could see.

Larry Love-Who-You-Are could see it, as he was now on hand and had headed straight to the O'Briens' after the sugar buffet. He was as happy as...well, as happy as Larry Love-Who-You-Are could be, to at last be able to tweak some changes that could help Bladen and Tim begin to feel happier about themselves and their lives.

Whilst both Bladen and Tim had been sleeping that night, Larry Love-Who-You-Are had bedded down on a soft towel in the bathroom which was situated opposite the twins' bedrooms. From there, he laid comfortably on his back with his arms crossed under his head and thought about what he could do to make this project work.

As soon as the twins had awoken that

morning, Larry Love-Who-You-Are was on duty and had spent the first eight minutes flitting between the two bedrooms to see how the day was beginning. Very quickly he could see the negative thought bubbles getting bigger and bigger and he wondered if he should do something that he had never done before.

He decided today was about doing, so he decided to give it a go!

First, he tiptoed into Bladen's room. There he was faced with an enormous, very sad bubble of beliefs. If he didn't get it soon, it might be too late. He positioned himself behind the thought bubble and began pushing with all his might.

This was harder than he thought but that only made him try harder. He pushed and pushed until Bladen's thoughts bubble had gone through the wall and was resting carefully on Tim's desk. He then did the same with Tim's bubble of feelings and pushed it firmly but gently (so as not to pop it and spill sad thoughts everywhere) into Bladen's room.

Phew, he had done it. He quickly checked the time. It was 7.19am. Mum would be in soon. He had just over 10 minutes to pop each bubble and allow Bladen and Tim to see exactly what the other was thinking and feeling.

Larry Love-Who-You-Are removed a wallet from his pocket and slid out a spangly gold pin. He peeped down at Bladen, who still had her eyes shut but managed to look very sad.

Three, two, one, pop! The thought bubble oozed Tim's thoughts out into Bladen's room. Thoughts never like to be exposed for too long, as it makes them feel unprotected. There is only one place that thoughts like to be, and that is inside the mind. So they scurried quickly to the first mind that they came upon...Bladen's!

Bladen opened her eyes with a start. Suddenly her mind had been swamped with feelings for Tim. For several moments, Bladen felt truly aware of how things felt inside of Tim's head. She had never realised how sad Tim was or how little he felt about himself; she always thought he was the okay twin.

Larry Love-Who-You-Are left Bladen thinking about what had just happened but needed to move quickly as he wasn't finished yet. With a quick step, he headed into Tim's bedroom where Bladen's thoughts were still intact. He plucked the pin out of his hat where he had placed it temporarily and burst the thought bubble.

Oh no, where was Tim? Why hadn't he checked the bed before he used the pin? Bladen's sad feelings were drifting around Tim's bedroom with nowhere to go. He heard a flush from the bathroom door that he hoped was Tim. He also heard movements from Mum and Dad's bedroom. The clock said 7.26am. Larry Love-Who-You-Are was now more than aware that Bladen's thoughts were going to head towards the first mind that they came across. Who was it going to be?

From each direction, footsteps could be heard. Larry Love-Who-You-Are was more nervous than he had ever been. How was he going to explain this to Chief Blink, problems on day one?!

The thoughts in Tim's bedroom were becoming restless. They had never been out of the safety of the brain for so long. Larry Love-Who-You-Are was stood as alert as could be, with pin still held tightly between thumb and forefinger, staring at the bedroom door.

At 7.29am Tim opened the door and threw himself into his bed for one last snuggle under the covers. Bladen's thoughts headed straight for his mind. Tim reacted just like Bladen and was suddenly perked up by the idea that Bladen wasn't perhaps as nasty as he thought she was. Maybe like him, she felt sad about herself a lot of the time too.

Maybe this was empathy, thought Tim. It had been talked about in an assembly the week before. Something about seeing things from another person's point of view, but he never really grasped it. Out of the blue, he felt that he could see things so clearly from inside Bladen's brain. If that wasn't seeing things from her point of view, he didn't know what was!

As the clock ticked over to 7.30am, Mrs O'Brien popped her head into Tim's room to give him the wake-up call. As she did, the last remaining thoughts gently seeped into Mum's mind. Her brain unexpectedly received two very alarming messages – *my life is pointless,* and *I hate feeling like this.*

Mum froze on the spot. Was this how Tim was feeling? She had never sensed it as strongly as she did at the moment she opened his bedroom door. What a horrible thought to know your child is feeling that sad. This was something she needed to talk to Reo about urgently.

She then popped her head into Bladen's

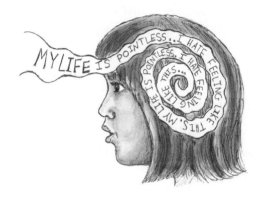

room to wake her up. As Mum saw her
lying there all scrunched up tightly in her
bed looking so fed up, it made her feel sad
too. The two thoughts popped back into
her head, *my life is pointless, I hate feeling
like this*. This time, they felt even stronger.
Were these to do with Bladen?

"Morning Bladen time to get up, are
you okay?" Bladen didn't answer but
just rolled back over to face the wall. She
wanted to hide, still feeling a bit nervous
that Mum might still be cross with her

after yesterday.

As Mum headed back towards her bedroom to get ready, she gave one last morning shout "Come on you two, today is a new day. Whatever happened yesterday is done. Hopefully, if you two can think about how the other person feels a little bit more, we might be able to move on from this."

Bladen and Tim were only too aware of what the other was feeling. They tried to distract themselves by quickly putting on their school uniforms and trying to shake off the strong feelings that were flooding their thoughts.

Mrs O'Brien sat on the side of the bed next to Mr O'Brien. "I am worried that Bladen isn't very happy at the moment."

"She's fine. She's just mean and nasty sometimes, as are all kids. Tim's no better at times, he can be horrible too. She'll get over it and she will learn eventually," replied Dad still half asleep.

"No, this isn't just meanness. I really think that she isn't happy, doesn't like her life, thinks it is pointless," said Mum feeling very troubled with what her mind was telling her.

"Don't get yourself in a pickle about this, love. We will talk to them after school and tell them we are fed up with the way they are behaving and treating each other, and us. Maybe we need to be tougher on them," stated Dad. "We will sort it."

"No Reo, this is different," continued Mum. "I feel like I have seen something very clearly this morning, it's like I saw inside their minds. Bladen isn't happy and we need to help her. Tim isn't happy either. Oh my goodness Reo, this is not about Bladen, it is about both of them. Our children don't feel good about themselves or their lives. We need to do something about this and quickly before more damage is done."

Chapter 5

Feelings are not always facts!

As everyone sat around the table having breakfast that morning, the mood felt different. Bladen and Tim weren't looking at each other. Although they were unaware that each other had experienced something similar that morning, knowing what they now knew made them feel very guilty for things that they had done in the past.

Mum was busy, busier than usual anyway. She couldn't shake the thoughts that had been implanted in her head that morning, and they were burying deeper and deeper into her mind. Her brain was also flooded with thoughts about her not being a good mum which was making her feel on edge. Had she failed her children? Was this her fault? How were she and Dad going to make this better?

Dad was the only one who was behaving normally. Although he had heard what Mrs O'Brien had said earlier, he perhaps hadn't given it the true attention it needed. He grabbed his bowl of cereal and cup of tea, then sat down in his usual seat.

"Morning, you two. It's very quiet, are you both okay? We would normally have had at least two arguments by now. In fact, something must definitely be the matter as I haven't heard either of you be mean to each other yet," said Dad jokingly.

Mum gave him a glare, which dad responded to with a shrug as if to say "Well, you wanted us to talk to them!"

Bladen and Tim both stopped. Dad was right. Pretty much every day, at least three or four times, the twins could be heard saying mean, hurtful things to each other. Mum and Dad had punished them, grounded them, taken screens away. They had lost pocket money, cinema trips, and new clothes. Nothing had seemed to work.

Yet today, the true reality of what they had been doing to each other and, more importantly, the impact it had been having was the hardest lesson of all. Neither of them replied.

"Listen, you two. This is important. Your Dad and I are worried that neither of you are as happy as we would like you to be. I had a really strong sensation this morning that I could read your thoughts.

Tim suddenly coughed muesli everywhere, completely shocked that Mum had experienced something similar to him. What was going on here? Bladen jumped up. She too had been surprised by what Mum had just said.

"Timeo, are you alright? I'll get some kitchen paper for you," said Bladen caringly.

"Timeo! Now I know that this is serious," responded Dad. "When do you ever call

Tim his real name? Tim the Wim....p maybe, but not Timeo!"

"Reo, you really aren't helping this morning. This is not the time to be making unkind jokes with the kids. What I said to you earlier was serious," shouted Mum.

Mum and Dad then broke off into an argument that left Bladen and Tim around the table.

"Thanks for getting the kitchen paper," started Tim.

"It's fine. Are you okay now? What

happened?" Bladen began to wonder if all three of them had experienced a similar thing that morning. But would Tim say?

"I was just a bit shocked that Mum wasn't having a go at us. It was unusual to hear her say that she felt like she could read our minds," said Tim while sharing full eye contact with Bladen.

"Yes, I know what you mean." Something about how Tim just looked at her, told her more than any of his words. Maybe this was a special twin thing.

"Do you think we can read each other's thoughts, Tim? You know, because we are twins?"

"Well, I have never thought it before, but I did feel it very strongly this morning. Just like Mum said, I felt that I saw some of your real feelings, Bladen,"

"Oh my goodness Tim, so did I. They were all sad thoughts though, about how much you don't like yourself, and I feel really guilty that that is because I have been so mean to you in the past."

"That is so weird. That is what I saw too. I think you are right, Bladen. It must have been a twin thing. Come on, let's get ready for school otherwise we will be late. We can talk about it on the way there."

As Bladen and Tim gathered their bags and coats, Mum and Dad were still arguing about what had happened earlier and whose approach had been the best.

"Bye, Mum. Bye, Dad," chorused the twins as they opened the door to leave.

"See you, kids. Have a good day!" echoed Mum and Dad.

As the door slammed behind them, Mum and Dad's arguing could be heard to be starting up again.

"I hate it when they argue. I always think it's my fault," said Bladen zipping up her coat.

"Yeh, me too. It is usually our fault though, isn't it?"

"Yes, I suppose it is. Maybe we should try harder to be more helpful to each other. I know I have been really horrible to you in the past, but you can be so annoying. Also, I always think Mum and Dad like you more than me."

"Really? Do you think that? I always think everyone likes you more than me. At least you are funny sometimes, I am just dull," said Tim, trying to hide his deeper feelings of sadness.

"You're not dull! Who told you that? It sounds like both of us might have got our facts wrong. Maybe we need to tell each other why we think our sad thoughts are not true. Shall we do it as a game?"

All the way to school Bladen and Tim talked openly about their thoughts and feelings, and it felt great. They answered negative thoughts with facts that could hopefully prove them wrong. What they realised more than anything was that a lot of what they had been feeling wasn't actually real.

What they hadn't realised was that thoughts are in fact just guesses. Lots and lots of the guesses that they had had in the past had been given too much of their attention, and so they both began to believe them. By playing the *'Where's the facts?'* game that morning, they were both already on the way to improving their self-esteem.

Larry Love-Who-You-Are beamed from inside the front mesh pocket of Tim's rucksack. He was so proud of Bladen and Tim. Never did he imagine that they would take this small act so seriously. The hardest part now was keeping them at it, but that would hopefully take some gentle nudging. He couldn't wait to share this success with Chief Blink at the midnight meeting later.

This was only the start for Larry Love-

Who-You-Are. Improving self-esteem was a big job that took time. He was also aware that Mum's self-esteem appeared to be a bit fragile at the moment too and so he needed to find a way to help her. She needed to know that she wasn't a bad mum. Maybe the twins could write her a letter, each telling her all the reasons why she was doing it well.

As Bladen and Tim arrived at school, a new sense of positivity filled their hearts. Never in their lifetime had they ever spent so long (and it was only a 15-minute walk) hearing such positive things about themselves. Normally, the twins had a sense of dread about school. A sense of nervousness was always present in their tummies, a fear that they would fail or get things wrong. This feeling was definitely weaker today.

As the children of Y6J filed into the cloakroom, bags and coats were hung onto pegs as if by magic. Tim's peg was right in the corner, furthest away from the classroom door and any escaping noise. Larry Love-Who-You-Are was content and comfortable. He decided that he would stay there for a while as he could afford to spend a couple of hours creatively resting (sleeping to you and me), hopeful that stage two of the project would be as satisfying as the first.

Fasten your seat-belts readers, the road ahead is going to be long and very, very bumpy.

Chapter 6

Caterpillars!

As Larry Love-Who-You-Are dreamed
peacefully of a good start, class Y6J
continued with their old ways. Very
quickly, Bladen and Tim's positivity
was seeping away. Grace, who sat on
Tim's table, was already dominating
the conversation with tales of dancing
competitions and distinctions. Tim
looked on, partly in frustration but also
in envy. What must it be like to be that
confident and have that much to say
about yourself? He looked at Stephen and
Charlie, who were not interested in any
way unlike Hannah, who appeared to be
in awe of Grace's magnificent talent and
who nodded and smiled in all the right
places to feed Grace's esteem. No-one even
seemed aware that he was there.

Bladen was having a very different experience on her table.

This is how the day usually started for Bladen. Lots and lots of unwanted attention, like being asked about ponies, what she did last night, who her best friend was and what score she got for her spelling test.

All of these questions were designed to make Bladen feel rubbish. And they did.

The pony incident had never left her, even though it had happened halfway through year two. She honestly thought it was going to stay with her forever. If ever a horse was mentioned at school, Bladen's name was muttered under people's breath and travelled directly into Bladen's ears. Teachers changed every year and so were unaware of Bladen's insignificant history. Sadly, her class remained the same and they still thrived on it.

The remaining questions were the same. What had she done last night? Well, that was easy. Nothing, because she never did anything cool or fun. Worse than that, she did nothing with anyone as she was an outcast amongst her class. Maggie had tried a few times to become friends with her, but Bladen was so nervous about it all going wrong that Maggie gave up.

What did you get on your spelling test? Bladen always got the lowest score. Not because she wasn't intelligent. No. It was because Bladen believed she was rubbish at everything and so wouldn't learn her spellings as she believed she would fail anyway, so what was the point?! This view is at the heart of low self-esteem. A belief that we are not good enough can become a message that runs through the core of us like a stick of rock! It was Larry Love-Who-You-Are's job to erase that message and create a new, more positive one.

Mrs Jackson started the day. "Good morning Y6J. You all look well this morning." She scanned her pupils and noticed a morsel of difference in Bladen and Tim. The grey cloud that normally lingered above them seemed to be brighter. She looked into Bladen's eyes. "I have a job that needs doing at lunch time, Bladen. Could you choose a friend and help me, please? You will get a queue jump pass to have your lunches first."

Everyone in the class threw their hands in the air and made agonising grunts in order to show that they wanted this special privilege the most. Bladen didn't know what to do. This had never happened to her before. She had never usually even put her hand up when this had happened in the past, knowing that she would never be selected. Who should she pick? Her mind was flooded with possibilities. In roughly five seconds, this is what went through Bladen's brain:

- Tim – her brother. Getting on better with him than ever. He also hates break times

- Evie Mae – could this be a chance to

repair a deeply damaged friendship?

- Maggie – she had tried several times to be friends with her but had stopped trying

- Sadaf – She was always kind to Bladen. Not because she liked Bladen any more than anyone else. Just because she was kind to everyone

"You obviously need a bit of time to think about it, Bladen. Let me know at the end of the second lesson," said Mrs Jackson.

The class slumped to normal positions.

"You'd better pick me," whispered Chante, the ring leader of all the negative attention that Bladen received every morning. Now Bladen had another choice:

- Chante – might be nice to me from now on if I pick her today

Yes, that was it. That choice had to be the one.

Although Bladen knew that Chante didn't deserve it, and she didn't really want to spend all lunchtime with someone she didn't like, it seemed to be the choice that might make things better in the future, so it was worth a go. She just needed to make sure Tim understood her reasoning.

During the morning lessons, Bladen's thoughts were ruled by the lunchtime job. She really wanted to pick Maggie. She felt that Maggie (who used to be quite mean to everyone in year five) deserved something positive back from Bladen. The friendship with Evie Mae could never be the same again. Evie Mae wasn't the forgiving type. Also, what about Tim? He had never been nicer to her than he was that morning. If she didn't pick him, he might hate her again. She really wished that she could talk to someone about this. Maybe she could ask Tim at break time.

Larry Love-Who-You-Are was suddenly jolted from a glorious sleep. He had been dreaming of honeysuckle and laughter. However, a sensation of negativity had awoken him and activated his brain into action. Bladen was in a dilemma, and he needed to help her. How could he do this at school? He checked his watch and noticed that it was 10 minutes until break time.

He needed to think quickly. How could he get Bladen alone, so that he could introduce himself and bat off the negativity of the day? Caterpillars! Yes, that was the answer! He quickly headed out towards the playing field.

At the top of the hill, a selection of trees lined the back fence. He knew that Bladen and Tim had regularly spent lots of miserable free time up there, sitting on the hill and watching everyone else having lots of playground fun. He felt confident that Bladen would take him there as they both knew that this time of year was when the caterpillars started to appear.

Larry Love-Who-You-Are got to work straight away. He removed a cloth bag from his pocket and collected lots of delicious juicy leaves that his trusted caterpillars could chomp on. When he felt confident that he had created a delicious feast, he hunted for as many caterpillars as possible who might like to join the party.

Just as the bell went for break time, Larry Love-Who-You-Are had carefully positioned eight rippling caterpillars who were beginning to tuck into the leafy banquet.

Bladen waited for Tim. "Tim, can I talk to you, please?"

"Can I talk to you later, Bladen?" asked Tim as he was running over to the concrete football pitch. "Robbie has asked me if I want to play footy today, so I am going to do it. See you later. Great that you got asked to do the job, by the way!"

Bladen's shoulders dropped. Suddenly a

hand tapped her on her sunken shoulder.

"You are going to pick me for the special job, aren't you?" ordered Chante.

"Errrrr, ermmmm, yes, I think so. Yes, of course. I will tell Mrs Jackson after break," muttered Bladen.

"Great, see you later," beamed Chante as she ran off towards her waiting friends.

Bladen put her head in her hands. At that moment, she felt totally lost. She dawdled to the only place in school that she ever felt safe. No-one went as far up the field as she did. No-one would come to look for her and there she could just be rubbish Bladen.

As she got closer to her favourite tree, she could see a flurry of movement from one of the lower branches. On closer inspection, Bladen could see an army of caterpillars munching away on a carefully gathered meal. As Bladen moved her head further towards them in wonder of nature in its natural form, a small voice was heard from a higher branch.

Bladen tilted her head in surprise.

"Hello, Bladen, I am so glad that you headed this way. This caterpillar celebration is just for you," began Larry Love-Who-You-Are.

As most children usually do in this situation, Bladen did the double blink gulp! "Are you talking? Are you talking...to me?" asked Bladen.

"Of course," replied Larry Love-Who-You-

Are. "As much as those green wrigglers are cute, they don't hold a good conversation. I am Blink 28770 Larry Love-Who-You-Are, and we are going to be working very closely together, Bladen because you don't seem as happy as you could be. Am I right?"

A ripple of emotions surged through Bladen. Sadness, uncertainty, excitement, relief and the most important one: hope. Could this tiny hat wearing creature, Larry Love-Who-You-Are, be her champion and help her move towards a better life, with happier feelings?

"I saw the emotions you felt just then, Bladen. I am glad that fear was not one of them. You really do not need to be scared. I have already been at work with you, Tim and your mum," continued Larry Love-Who-You-Are.

"Was that you? You helped us see things from each other's point of view? Wow, that is amazing. How did you do that?" asked

Bladen excitedly.

"I can tell you that another time. We need to work fast. Larry Love-Who-You-Are looked at his watch. "We have eight minutes and I believe that you have a dilemma that needs urgent attention. Come on, let's sit on the hill."

Bladen held out her hand in gratitude

and Larry Love-Who-You-Are tiptoed from the branch onto her welcoming hand.

"So, Bladen, first I need to tell you about a couple of Blink rules. One is that you must share your difficulties with an adult that you trust so that you are not alone after we finish and two, the Blinks' magic must always stay between just you and me," said Larry Love-Who-You-Are. He then went on to tell several stories of children in the past who created some very difficult situations by talking about the Blinks' help! "Are you okay with that?"

"Of course," said Bladen nodding seriously.

"Brilliant. Now you can tell me about your situation and let's see what we can do about it."

"Well…" began Bladen nervously.

Chapter 7

Selfishness

Larry Love-Who-You-Are listened intently as Bladen told of her life and the feelings of failure that she felt most of the time. On top of that, she now had the nightmare of having been picked for a job and worse still having to do it with Chante!

Every second that Bladen talked, she noticed that she felt lighter. What she was most amazed at was that break time was only 15 minutes in total, and yet she already felt like she had been talking to Larry Love-Who-You-Are for hours. This situation in itself already seemed quite bizarre, so it would not have surprised her in the slightest if Larry Love-Who-You-Are had some magical power of being able to slow down time.

As she chattered away, Larry Love-Who-You-Are was writing things down in the small notepad he had taken out from under his hat.

"What are you writing?" asked Bladen.

"Oh sorry, did that put you off? While I am listening, I note down the important things that you are saying, things that I think I can help you with and things that we can do together to make this situation better. Please carry on," replied Larry Love-Who-You-Are.

"What can I do about this job I've been asked to do? I have had to pick Chante as she would make my life a misery if I didn't," probed Bladen.

"It sounds like Chante makes you unhappy already, Bladen and is only one of many things that make your life a misery. This is the first thing that we need to do together - challenge some of your fears. Could she really be as unkind as you think she might be? What is the worst that she could do if you said no?" tested Larry Love-Who-You-Are.

"She would be meaner to me," said Bladen.

"She already is mean, and that is wrong. You need to think more about yourself, Bladen and start to stick up for yourself," responded Larry Love-Who-You-Are.

"No way would I dare shout at or challenge Chante. She is much stronger than me, and I am rubbish at anything like that. I would do it all wrong and make it worse," said Bladen.

"Sticking up for yourself isn't about shouting at people, or being rude and angry. It is about being true to how you feel and saying it confidently. It is like having someone on your side and that someone is you!" answered Larry Love-Who-You-Are.

Bladen liked that idea. A best friend within her all the time. But that sounded easier than it would be, surely?

"Do you want to do the job with Chante?" asked Larry Love-Who-You-Are.

"No way! I only said yes so that she might be nice to me. I don't even think that she would be, even if I did. Then I would feel even guiltier for not picking Maggie, who I really want. Or Tim, who I feel I should pick. I really wish the teacher hadn't picked me," said Bladen, feeling almost teary.

"Okay, so you pick Maggie. Maggie is who you would like and who will make the special job even better. You might not be picked again for a long time, Bladen, so you need to make sure that you make this experience as brilliant as possible," nodded Larry Love-Who-You-Are.

"What about Chante? What if it upsets Tim?" queried Bladen.

"Chante won't like it. Of course she won't. But, you doing what you feel is right for you shows real strength of character. Even if you feel weaker than a woodlouse, sometimes we just have to do it and pretend it until we feel it for real," answered Larry Love-Who-You-Are.

"It feels selfish. I always feel guilty if I am being selfish. That is why I try to do what other people want all the time. That is why I feel I have to pick Chante," said Bladen.

"Thinking about what you want is not being selfish, Bladen. It is how we do something that makes an act selfish or not. If we do what we want all the time and don't care about how it makes others feel, or deliberately hurt people's feelings, then yes we are being selfish," began Larry Love-Who-You-Are.

"However, by remembering that we are important too and are allowed to live the life that we would like, gives us a role in the choices that we make. The difference between bad selfish and good selfish is the fact that we consider and care how other people might feel. At the moment Bladen, you think about everyone else too much and not about yourself at all, which affects your self-esteem," continued Larry Love-Who-You-Are.

"Wow, that is good. I like that. So I wouldn't be selfish if I asked Maggie? But what about Tim?" sighed Bladen.

"Tim might be upset or he might not. Hopefully, he is having a great playtime playing football with Robbie and the boys. He was positively selfish when you wanted to talk. He wanted to play football as he isn't asked very often. He had to make the most of the opportunity, didn't he? If he had talked to you instead, he would have felt annoyed at himself and at you for stopping him from doing what he really wanted to do, so neither of you would have had a good playtime. Now you both are having a good time!" exclaimed Larry Love-Who-You-Are.

"Yes, I see that. I could always explain what you have just told me about selfishness too. I think he would like that, and we could agree to do that more for each other in the future," pondered Bladen.

"Great idea," said Larry Love-Who-You-Are and held his hand up for a high-five. "Right, we have one minute left and we need a script to tell Chante.

Bladen's tummy flipped over. This wasn't going to go well. She already had the familiar feeling in difficult situations that she just wanted to run away and hide until it was all over.

"You can do this, Bladen, I believe in you. We never know what we can do until we try. When something is difficult Bladen, we don't give up, we try harder," stated Larry Love-Who-You-Are.

"I never do difficult things, I always give up, is that another reason why my self-esteem is low?" asked Bladen.

"Yes! It is the hardest things in life that teach us the most about who we are and what we can do. Do you want your life to be happier?" started Larry Love-Who-You-Are.

"Of course," replied Bladen.

"Are you ready to make changes to your life for the better?"

"I am," echoed Bladen with a new found sense of determination.

"What are you going to tell Chante?" asked Larry Love-Who-You-Are.

"Well, first I am going to ask Maggie if she would like to help me. If she says yes then that will spur me on to tell Chante," began Bladen.

The end of playtime bell rang from the playground.

"Oh no," said Bladen.

"Come on, I will come with you to

the classroom. What could you say to Chante?" reminded Larry Love-Who-You-Are.

"How about...I am sorry Chante, but I have picked Maggie to help with the job this lunchtime, as she has been so kind to me lately, I wanted to do something nice for her too. Hope you understand. Oh, and by the way Chante, I don't like it when you are mean to me. If you don't stop it I am going to tell the teacher," chanted Bladen, shocked by this new her.

Larry Love-Who-You-Are danced around on Bladen's hand. He couldn't have been more proud but better than that, neither could Bladen. Even though she was highly nervous about what she needed to do, she was going to do it this new way and see what happened.

"There's Maggie," said Larry Love-Who-You-Are pointing towards the outside of the huts.

"How do you know Maggie?" asked Bladen.

"We Blinks know lots of things," said Larry Love-Who-You-Are with a cheeky wink. "Do you want me to stay with you while you do this or do you want me to go? An audience can make it worse."

"Oh please stay," pleaded Bladen.

"Okay" replied Larry Love-Who-You-Are. "But, although you have me on your side, the most important person to be your best support is you."

"Just for these two things, please. Knowing you are there will make me feel stronger. Thank you," said Bladen revving herself up for what she needed to do. "Maggie," she shouted.

"Hi Bladen! Where have you been this break time? I wanted to give you an invitation to my party on Saturday," chirped Maggie.

A ripple of loveliness erupted inside Bladen. This was going to be so easy. "Would you like to help me with the special job at lunchtime today?"

"Oooh yes please Bladen, that would be brill," smiled Maggie. "I thought Chante was doing it? Well, that's what she has been telling everyone this playtime anyway."

"Yes, she is…she was. Only because she told me I had to pick her. I said yes to keep her happy but then I realised that I would be unhappy. I want to enjoy this chance and I know I will with you,

Maggie," said Bladen honestly. The girls walked into the classroom.

"Is she mean to you a lot, Bladen?" asked Maggie while getting her pencil case out of her drawer ready to take to maths.

"Yes. But I let her do it. I never stick up for myself or tell her to stop," replied Bladen.

"Do you want me to do it? I will stick up for you and give her a mouthful at the same time," ranted Maggie in a way that Bladen hadn't seen for a while.

"Thanks, Maggie but I am going to tell her myself. I need to do this."

"Okay but if you need back-up, you know where I am," smiled Maggie.

Bladen sat down on her table. Luckily Chante was already there and the rest of the table were still hanging up coats.

"Chante, can I have a word?" began Bladen.

As she delivered her script, Chante's face went from annoyingly smug to disbelief. "Oh yes and if you keep saying unkind things to me I will be telling Mrs Jackson from now on, okay?" said Bladen with a fire in her belly that felt good.

Before Chante could reply, Mrs Jackson was sending everyone to their maths groups. Chante was fuming, but in a way that made Bladen feel that she had done this right. Maggie had been watching from across the room and put a 'thumbs up'.

Larry Love-Who-You-Are had been right. We don't know what we can do until we try. That had been hard to do but the feelings after were some of the best feelings ever. Then from inside Bladen's skirt pocket, she felt a fluttering, bouncing feeling. It was Larry Love-Who-You-Are's dance of success, and that too made what she had done all the more worthwhile.

Chapter 8

Bad news

As Bladen and Tim were walking home from school, both agreed that lots of good things had happened that day. Tim had enjoyed the game of football with Robbie and the boys and had even managed to set up a good goal for Asif, which went down well.

If he was honest, a bit of him had been upset that Bladen hadn't picked him for the job, especially as they seemed to be getting on better than ever before. However, he knew that Bladen had never really recovered from the fake pony saga and her friendships, or lack of them, reminded her daily. A friend was what she needed more than anything and as her brother, he wanted that for her too.

Tim surprised himself with what he had just been thinking. This time last year, last month or even last week, a situation like this would have made him feel deeply rejected and angry. Maybe it was because he saw things more clearly now, or that he had more caring feelings for Bladen. He couldn't help but feel that it was also the fact that he had done something good that day, and that made him feel good.

Robbie had been asking Tim to play footie at break times for a while, but Tim's negative thinking always kicked in and stopped him. This wasn't unusual for Tim. He did this with pretty much everything. Does this sound like someone you know?

Tim never learned his spellings as he thought he would get them all wrong, so what was the point? He never put his hand up as he didn't think he knew any right answers. He never tried to make friends with people as he thought they wouldn't like him anyway. But most often he felt lonely, rejected and a failure.

Although he had some of those familiar feelings after Bladen picked Maggie, what was different today was that they were less strong. What was also different was that he didn't want to punish Bladen for not picking him. This was what normally happened in the O'Brien household. Bladen upset Tim, then he saved it up and used it against her in the future and vice versa. But that urge wasn't there today. In fact, he was genuinely quite interested to know how it had gone.

"How did the job go today? What did you have to do?" asked Tim.

"It was great! We both got to have an early lunch so everything was nice and hot and not dried up and crunchy! We had to carefully cut out all the artwork that we have done on 'landscapes' so that Mrs Jackson could do a display. Maggie was brilliant. We even had a good laugh," said Bladen happily.

"I heard Chante wasn't happy about it.

She was really mad when we were queuing up for lunch, and she could see you and Maggie enjoying your puddings," explained Tim.

"I know. She told me I had to pick her or else, but I changed my mind and did what I felt was right not what I felt I had to do. She even came into the classroom over lunch and challenged me," whispered Bladen.

Tim gasped. "No way, what happened?"

"Well, first I just listened. Then I told her if she was kinder, people might ask her because she was nice and not because she forced people into doing it."

"What did she say?" asked Tim eagerly.

"She didn't say anything. Maggie then started clapping which took her by surprise and then she left, just as Mrs Jackson was coming in to see if we were okay. Chante then got told off for being in the classroom without permission," said Bladen with a satisfied smile on her face. "Even better, we were told that we had worked so hard and done such a good job we can be lunchtime monitors whenever jobs are needed in the future. You didn't mind me picking Maggie, did you?"

"I did a bit but only because you are my sister and everyone always wants to be picked. But I had a great thing happen to me at break time with the football, and so it was your turn," said Tim, nervously wondering if he had been too honest and made Bladen feel bad.

"Thanks Tim, that means a lot. I owe you one, and you can call it in at any time," answered Bladen with a genuine smile.

As the children walked home, they talked and talked about their day. The hardest part of the day so far was not being able to share with Tim what had happened with Larry Love-Who-You-Are. She knew he wouldn't believe her anyway, but more importantly she wanted Larry Love-Who-You-Are to stay around for a lot longer. But telling would end the Blink magic straight away.

As they arrived home, they went straight around the back as usual. The gate was locked, and neither Tim nor Bladen could open the high bolt. They went back to the front and knocked on the door. Something was not right. They looked at each other as they heard footsteps coming along the hallway.

Mum answered the door her face red and swollen from crying.

"Come in, kids. Go into the living room. There is something that I need to tell you," said Mum doing her best to hold it together.

"Mum what is it? Tell us," said Bladen and Tim in chorus.

Mum started sobbing again. Huge tears popped out of her eyes and were quickly mopped up with a scrunched up ball of toilet tissue.

"Your dad and I are going to have a break from each other. He is going to stay at Grandma and Grandad's for a while so we can have some time to think," explained Mum.

Bladen burst out crying "Are you getting divorced?"

"Hopefully, it won't come to that. We have just been arguing a lot lately and we can't agree on something that I feel is very important, so we need some time apart," said Mum.

"Is this our fault?" asked Tim.

"No. I just feel your dad and I need to work more as a team, and he is so busy that he doesn't always understand that," answered Mum between sniffs.

"It *is* our fault then. That is what you were arguing about this morning!" shouted Bladen and ran into her bedroom.

Tim wasn't sure what to do.

"Please, you two. Let's not have this, not today anyway. It will get sorted. I just need some time. Your dad is picking you up from school on Friday and taking you both to Grandma and Grandad's for the weekend," stated Mum firmly.

Tim decided it was best for him to leave and go to his bedroom too. As he went up the stairs, he could hear Bladen sobbing from inside her room. Normally he would leave her as it wasn't worth trying to help.

What he felt today was a day of doing things differently. He gave a gentle knock.

"Go away," bellowed Bladen.

"It's me. Do you want me to come in?" asked Tim.

"Why would I want you to do that? I hate you. This is all your fault," screeched Bladen.

Tim felt wounded. How could she think that he was responsible for all this? He ran into his bedroom, slammed the door and threw himself onto his bed in a flood of angry tears.

Larry Love-Who-You-Are peeped through his hands from the top of Tim's wardrobe. This was not part of the plan. He had not seen this coming. Suddenly he too was filled with self-doubt. Should he have done more work with Mum and Dad today rather than with Bladen? Was this project too much? Could he make this better when it seemed to be getting worse? What was he going to say to Chief Blink?

Larry Love-Who-You-Are then decided to say to himself what he had been telling Bladen to do all break time. He was not going to give up, no way. This was going to make him work harder. He was going to make this better, as better as possible. Bladen and Tim deserved that. He decided that now was not a good time to do anything with the twins or Mum. They needed time to get their heads around the bad news of the day.

What he needed to do was much more important. He needed an urgent meeting with Chief Blink and midnight was too long away. He needed to do something now.

Chapter 9

Action plan

Larry Love-Who-You-Are tiptoed out of the O'Brien's house wondering how he could possibly find Chief Blink before the hour of midnight. Where would you spend your day time if you were a very important Blink who no longer worked on projects during the daytime? He reminded himself of what he liked to do when he was in the 'Whey hey' stage. In the past Larry Love-Who-You-Are had been known to:

- watch many ice hockey games

- sneak into the cinema and watch superhero films

- travel to the nearest seaside to breathe in the wonderful, fresh, salty air

- bed down in hanging baskets (spring

and summer only) for a mammoth sleep

- craft super-fast sledges and speed down unused snowy hills

But what might Chief Blink do? Larry Love-Who-You-Are wondered if the local library might be an option as it would be peaceful and calm. Maybe the Wise Ones had a special home or office, but he would struggle to find that this afternoon. The only place that he felt held any clues was Rosie's Bakery and so off he headed.

On his way, Larry Love-Who-You-Are scanned every area for Chief Blink, or in fact any Blink, who might be able to help him at this important time. As he passed the sports field, he spotted Blink 14711 Grace-Go-For-It perched on the top of the rugby post. He headed over in the hope that she might know something that could help him on his mission.

"Hi Grace-Go-For-It how are you today?" asked Larry Love-Who-You-Are.

"Good thanks and how are you? I haven't seen you for ages. It is a long time since we have been at the same stage of a project together. I am in the 'Eye Spy' stage at the moment, and luckily everything is going as planned so hopefully in a few more days, I can begin the Blink fun time!" said Grace-Go-For-It with an excited smile. "What stage are you in?"

"I am very much in the 'Help' stage. In fact, I don't think I have ever needed more help than I do at this moment. I am working with twins on this project which makes it hard enough, but now their Mum and Dad have just split up," began Larry Love-Who-You-Are. "Chief Blink once had a situation that involved twins and so has offered to help me with this one."

"Wow. That is a real honour," commented Grace-Go-For-It. "I didn't know Chief Blink did that, I heard that she spends most of her time doing Sudoku these days."

"Really, do you know where?" asked Larry Love-Who-You-Are hopeful this might lead him in the right direction.

"No, sorry. Though Blink 10268 Callum-Committed writes them for her as part of his Wise One role and I have seen him at the boating lake hut in the park.

"Great. Thank you so much Grace-Go-For-It, you have really helped. Good luck with your last few days and see you soon," shouted Larry Love-Who-You-Are already off in the distance.

On his way, Larry Love-Who-You-Are was thinking about what he thought he needed to do for Bladen and Tim. Although he felt desperate for Chief Blink's wisdom on this one, he knew that it would not be fair or satisfying to ask her to do all the work. He needed a plan for her agree with or tweak if necessary. So what was his action plan going to be?

He knew that the work on self-esteem was still desperately needed but he also now felt that the surprise separation of their parents was going to take a lot of input, not just for Bladen and Tim but also for Mum and Dad. Larry Love-Who-You-Are couldn't help but feel that if he helped Dad change his mind about a few of the things that were upsetting Mrs O'Brien, then that could help all of them. Yes, that was his plan, to start with Dad.

Before he knew it, Larry Love-Who-You-Are was entering the park gates. As it was a school day, the park was quite quiet and most of the mums and toddlers were enjoying lunch in the café. Yet parks were places where Blinks had been spotted before. More than one Blink in the past had been sniffed out by dogs or children and ended up in the river or worse still, clamped tightly in the hands of sticky little fingers!

Larry Love-Who-You-Are scampered towards the boating lake hut. As he expected the hut was securely locked, only open on weekends and school holidays. So if Callum-Committed were here, he would have to be on the outside somewhere. Larry Love-Who-You-Are gave a gentle shout "Callum Committed, are you there?" He moved around the hut. No sign on the roof. No Callum-Committed on the ledges of any of the windows. In fact, no sign at all. Then Larry Love-Who-You-Are spotted a tiny scrap of paper with what looked a grid marked upon it. He picked it up and felt confident that it was the edge of a Sudoku puzzle. Callum-Committed had been here. Maybe he still was.

"Callum-Committed, are you here? I

need your help," shouted Larry Love-Who-You-Are again slightly louder this time, but there was no response. He tucked the piece of paper into his pocket and with a sigh, decided that the bakery was the only other choice he had.

As he was heading out of the park and over the woods, Larry Love-Who-You-Are noticed another piece of paper, the same as he had had in his pocket up in one of the trees. Callum-Committed must definitely have been here, but when? He decided to shout his name again "Callum-Committed? It is me Larry Love-Who-You-Are. I would really like to talk to you if you are free?"

Still nothing.

He continued on his way. He then saw another piece of paper and another. They were getting closer together and nearer and nearer to the large collection of heron nests. "Callum-Committed, can you hear me? It is Larry Love-Who-You-Are. Are you in trouble?"

Still no response. However, Larry Love-Who-You-Are did have a strong feeling in his tummy that something wasn't right. He decided that he needed to brave the rookery. First, he moved towards the empty nests, but there was no sign of any Blink life. Then he gently tiptoed towards the busy nests. This was scary. A heron could easily pop him into its mouth, and he would be out of action for a considerable amount of time. This was the last thing he needed, especially with the case he was working on. He decided to take a risk.

Out from under his hat, Larry Love-Who-You-Are removed a harmonica and blew a high-pitched sound at full blast. He was instantly faced with the loud flapping of wings and a huge draught which blew him backwards off the branch and into a nest several metres below. He quickly pulled himself together as he knew that time was against him; the herons wouldn't leave their rookery free for too long.

He moved from one nest to the other checking under eggs with his gloved hands so not to leave any scent. Then he saw him. Callum-Committed was fast asleep on a soft feather bed. "Hey Callum-Committed, are you okay?" asked Larry Love-Who-You-Are gently shaking him by the arm.

"Whoooaahh," said Callum-Committed with a start. "What? Where? Why?"

"You have been asleep in this heron's nest. I am not sure why but I found some of your scraps of paper and they led me here," began Larry Love-Who-You-Are.

"Larry Love-Who-You-Are, thank you. You have saved me. Yes, I remember now. I have been here many hours. One of the herons picked me up in its beak and brought me to her nest. She has no eggs as you can see so I think she hoped that I might hatch and become her own chick. She has been sat on me for hours and I couldn't escape. That was when I released the paper in the hope someone might find me if they needed me. Very quickly though, I fell asleep. The truth is that it was so warm and cosy there, I allowed myself to drift off and have a snooze!" explained Callum-Committed with slightly flushed cheeks. "Anyway, why did you end up over this way?"

"I am hoping that you can help me. I desperately need to find Chief Blink as she is helping with my project and it has just become even more difficult. Do you know where she might be at the moment?" asked Larry Love-Who-You-Are with fingers crossed behind his back.

"Oh dear! This is a real dilemma as once we become a Wise One, we must keep certain information secret. Chief Blink's whereabouts is one of them," answered Callum-Committed.

Larry Love-Who-You-Are put his head in his hands again, which was becoming the norm.

"Okay. Listen. You head towards the bakery, and I will head straight over to Chief Blink and explain that you need to see her urgently. Oh and thank you for finding me, it is always good to know help is at hand," smiled Callum-Committed heading off to where he needed to be.

"Thank you too. I will see you later," said Larry Love-Who-You-Are, who then moved spritely in the opposite direction towards Rosie's Bakery. What an interesting day today was turning out to be, he thought.

Chapter 10

Power

Larry Love-Who-You-Are had only just arrived in the bakery when Chief Blink gently put her hand on his shoulder. "I understand that you have hit some greater challenges with your project. Come on, let's perch out the back where it is quieter." Chief Blink guided Larry Love-Who-You-Are into the back room and they settled down into the dishcloths that were neatly folded on one of the higher shelves.

"Thank you so much for your time and support with my project, Chief Blink. Yes you are right, having twins is tough. Both Bladen and Tim are great children, but their many qualities get hidden under the grey blanket of sadness that they carry around themselves. Neither of them sees themselves as the good person they actually are. They are also so caught up in their negative self, that they can be very unkind to each other too. These cruel messages make both of them feel even more sad about who they are and so they don't always make the right choices. I feel that they are on a rollercoaster ride which only goes down and doesn't have any good parts," explained Larry Love-Who-You-Are.

"Yes, when you take the low self-esteem ride there is little joy. Sad thoughts about yourself make you feel miserable and then you behave as you feel - sad, uncaring, a failure, and angry. Poor Bladen and Tim, they are two of many kids who might feel like this at times. However, with some work and practice, things can change. Are the twins ready for things to be better?" asked Chief Blink.

"Yes, Chief Blink. Very definitely, yes. Bladen and Tim swapped thought bubbles yesterday and saw the realities of how each other really felt. Even Mum got a chance to see the reality of how the twins were feeling. All three of them were quite shocked, but this made them take each other more seriously and make more effort to be kind. However, Mum and Dad have now split up because they are arguing all the time over the twins. Dad thinks they are naughty and need punishing, and Mum thinks they need more help and support. So this really is a tough one," continued Larry Love-Who-You-Are.

"Mmm, so what are you thinking Larry Love-Who-You-Are?" asked Chief Blink.

"Well, because the twins are with Mum, I feel that it is Mum at the moment who could do the most to help the twins. I know that Dad needs some input too, but maybe he can wait," pondered Larry Love-Who-You-Are.

"What do you feel is causing the biggest problem in this situation, Larry Love-Who-You-Are?" asked Chief Blink.

"Well, I suppose Dad, as he doesn't understand the reality of the situation and so what he does and says is making the problem worse," began Larry Love-Who-You-Are. "So do you think I need to start with him?"

"I am not here to tell you what to do, Larry Love-Who-You-Are. I am here to support you through whatever decisions you make. Sometimes we all feel that we have to make the totally best choices in life for things to be good. That is a challenge in itself. As long as the choice we make is good enough, then things will also be okay and it removes all that pressure and stress that we put on ourselves for perfection. Perfection rarely exists but much wonderfulness is always available for the taking. Are you ready to take yours?" asked Chief Blink.

Larry Love-Who-You-Are was thinking long and hard. What Chief Blink had just said was so right. Not just for him in how he moved this project forward, but also for the twins and in fact, for everyone. "Thank you Chief Blink, you have been really helpful. I suppose when anyone is faced with a problem or new challenge they feel nervous but like you said, it is about doing something good enough, and that feels very powerful," reflected Larry Love-Who-You-Are.

"Exactly, Larry Love-Who-You-Are. I needed to do this exercise with you today for you to realise the importance of personal power which is hidden away in everyone. Once you unlock it, you feel like someone is on your side all the time. The best thing is, that person is you! You become your own best friend and these small changes help us believe we are okay, we can do, and more importantly, we can cope with setbacks as *'part'* of everyday life rather than feeling they are the *'whole'* thing. Does that make sense?" asked Chief Blink.

"Yes. Wow, you have taught me so much. I feel so much more confident now within myself. I was feeling better before because I had you as my guide but now you have

helped me understand that the answers
are always within me. This is what I need
to do with Bladen and Tim, and with Mum
and Dad too, isn't it?" confirmed Larry
Love-Who-You-Are.

"Well done, Larry Love-Who-You-Are.
You are a very smart Blink. I have seen
you grow so much in the short space
of this journey so far. I look forward to
seeing and hearing about your further
developments. Here is my whistle." Chief
Blink handed Larry Love-Who-You-Are
an old fashioned, black football referee's
whistle. "Keep this safe. You may use this

at any point throughout this project for

me to come to you. However, remember
that I am not here to give answers so,
if you blow the whistle and you haven't
thought of good enough choices, it will not
work. Good luck. I will see you later at the
midnight meeting."

Larry Love-Who-You-Are slipped the
whistle into his inside pocket. Knowing
that he had it made him feel more capable,
which he thought must be part of the
plan. Now he needed to get on with what
was best to do next. He stopped for a
minute. Suddenly he remembered that the
twins were due to go to Dad's in two days.
If he didn't start working on Dad, then the
weekend could make things even worse.
Also, Bladen had an invite to Maggie's
party, and it was very important that she
went to it.

Although Larry Love-Who-You-Are knew
that Mum and Dad both needed some
input, he decided to head to Dads. He felt
that some positive action there and a bit
of time for it to settle in, could actually

make the biggest and best difference to everything, especially the weekend ahead. He checked his watch, it was 6.44pm. If he acted quickly, he would be able to do what he needed to do. He set to work.

By the time he was finished it was 7.18pm. This was perfect timing for what he had in mind. He headed towards Mr O'Brien's parents' house just in time to catch him drifting into his post-dinner snooze.

Larry Love-Who-You-Are loved a bit of dream tweaking. However, the timing was essential. He wanted to implant a dream sequence early on in the sleep cycle so that it felt more like an experience than a dream. Mr O'Brien was breathing heavier and so his brain was slowing down. The next move needed to be very gentle and careful.

As Larry Love-Who-You-Are balanced on the side of Mr O'Brien's ear, he noticed that he was moving up and down due to his breathing. This was no good. He could easily mess up if he didn't get this right. He moved to the cushion that propped up Mr O'Brien's head. This was too far. Suddenly Larry Love-Who-You-Are remembered what Chief Blink had said earlier that day, *'it doesn't need to be perfect, just good enough'*. The cheek was the better option. He parted his legs slightly so that he felt more stable. The breathing was getting deeper and deeper. He then reduced himself to as small as he could go. He moved into Mr O'Brien's ear cavity where he removed a tiny cartridge which was made of the thinnest paper imaginable.

This was why he had to be careful. The cartridge contained many thoughts of Bladen and Tim. It included feelings and memories. It also included the reality of the future if things weren't changed soon. If the paper tore, everything would escape into the air and not into Mr O'Brien's dream zone. Larry Love-Who-You-Are tapped the wall of Dad's ear. A small flap opened up. He carefully inserted the special package and tapped the wall again. The cartridge disappeared.

Larry Love-Who-You-Are moved out of the inner ear and perched back onto the orange cushion and waited. He had only done this method once or twice before but it had always been successful. The cartridge acted like a script that the imagination then brought to life to create a dream-like film. After five minutes Mr O'Brien began shuffling and grunting. This was a good sign. The dream film was stirring his emotions.

Mr O'Brien slept for roughly 22 minutes. Perfect. As he awoke, his face looked heavy. His eyes looked sad. He sat up with a start. "Tim, Bladen, come here please," he shouted.

"They aren't here Reo, you have just woken up," called his mum from the kitchen. "Did you dream they were here?"

"I need to go and see them straight away. That wasn't a dream. I will be back later," explained Reo pulling on his shoes and heading towards the door.

"Are you doing the right thing, Reo?" yelled his mum.

This had never felt more right, ever, thought Dad as he jumped into the car.

Chapter 11

Opposites

Larry Love-Who-You-Are was also heading towards the O'Briens', hopeful that Dad was going to use this new found information about the twins and make things better. As he arrived there, the mood in the house was low, very low.

Mum was in the living room staring at the television screen, watching it but not taking in any information. Her brain was too busy with all the things that were flooding through her mind. Bladen had stopped crying but was still red-eyed and beginning to feel pangs of hunger, having been up in her room since coming in from school. Tim was angry. He had spent the last few hours punching his pillow and even hurt his foot after kicking his bin across the room. Initially, he was cross that Bladen could blame him for all this, but after the hours had ticked away, he was now furious because he believed that it was all his fault. Although he had registered the lack of food several hours ago, the deep emotions in his tummy were holding his hunger pangs away.

A loud knocking sound suddenly jerked all three of them out of their distant selves. Mum jumped up and headed to the door.

As she opened the door, Mr O'Brien was standing there with his head in his hands. "This is a mess. You were right, I need to see Bladen and Tim. I am always so busy with work that I don't think I have seen the reality of how little they feel about themselves. Where are they? I need to see them. Can I come in?" said Dad unable to hide his sad feelings.

Mrs O'Brien started to cry again, but the

tears suddenly turned to anger. "So you think you have the magic wand to make all this better, do you? This isn't going to be fixed because you suddenly understand it. We have a lot of work to do, and that is going to be harder now that you have moved out," cried Mum wiping tears from her reddened cheeks.

"Our arguing all the time can't be helping. I don't think that the twins seeing us at our worst with each other can make them feel happy. We just need a break in order to realise what we want. If we aren't happy, how can the kids be?" explained Dad.

"We do need to make sure that we let them know it is not because of them. I felt that when my mum and dad split up. I really don't want them to feel what I felt then. Can you do that?" asked Mum with uncertainty.

"Of course I will. They are with me this weekend and I will make sure we have some quality time together. I can't remember the last time I spent quality time with either of them. I always thought we had lots of time milling around the house together, and that was enough," defended Dad, who was now riddled with guilt. He couldn't remember the last time he had played football in the garden with Tim or played his and Bladen's favourite game – sock wrestling!

"Oh, and Bladen has a party this weekend which you will need to take her to," said Mum.

Dad felt wounded. He wanted so desperately to have the time with Bladen this weekend. "She needs to spend the time with me. I am going to plan some lovely things. She can go to a party anytime," started Dad. Then he remembered the dream. Bladen never got invited to parties as she had very few friends. This was not about him, it was about Bladen. She would enjoy the party. She needed friends. As much as it hurt him, he knew that he needed to do this for Bladen. "Actually, forget all that, of course I will take her to the party."

Mum looked shocked. This was a turnaround. She took the invitation out of Bladen's bag and handed it to Reo. "I will organise the card and present, you just need to drop her off and pick her up from Maggie's house," said Mum. "I think we should talk to the twins together now, as they need to know that this isn't about them. Agreed?"

"Agreed," said Dad shocked by how connected to the family he felt, even though he was now more physically apart. Larry Love-Who-You-Are did an excited clap to himself. So far, so good.

Mum headed upstairs followed by Larry Love-Who-You-Are. She spoke outside both their doors. "Bladen, Tim, your dad is here. We would like to talk to you both. Can you come downstairs, please? This is important. I know you are both feeling upset, so are we, but hopefully your dad and I can help you to understand this a little bit better. You must be starving, both of you. I will make up some cream cheese bagels; they will be ready in five minutes."

Bladen's tummy perked to life at the thought of food. Although she didn't want to go downstairs at all, the temptation of toasted bagels with soft cream cheese melting down the sides pulled her towards the door. Tim wanted to go downstairs more than ever but wasn't sure if he could hide the anger he was still feeling, and not even a bagel could change that.

Tim heard Bladen's door opening. Would she go down on her own? Might she knock for him? Did he want her to knock for him? He was still mad at what she had said earlier. Although the smell of warm bagels was wafting up the stairs, Bladen didn't feel that she could head downstairs alone. She knocked on Tim's door.

"Tim, are you coming down to see Mum

and Dad?" asked Bladen.

"Not with you I'm not," snapped Tim, who really wanted this to be over but as usual kept it going a bit longer.

"I'm sorry for what I said earlier, I didn't mean it. I was so upset with what Mum said about Dad. I have been crying for the last few hours. Please, can we do this together? I am just going to wash my face," said Bladen.

Tim wanted to go but felt like if he did, then Bladen would be let off the hook and so she would win. Larry Love-Who-You-Are suddenly thought about self-esteem being about personal power; it's not about winning, it is about what feels better for you. Better still if both sides feel better, then win-win!

"Why aren't you going with her?" asked Larry Love-Who-You-Are perched on top of Tim's bent knee.

Tim did the usual response of *'gulp gulp*

blink' when he saw Larry Love-Who-You-Are in front of him. "What is this? Who are you?" asked Tim.

"I am Blink 28770 Larry Love-Who-You-Are, and I have been working with your family over the last few days, as neither you nor Bladen seem to be as happy as you could be. Am I right?"

"Yes. Yes you are. I don't think I have liked me or my life for ages but weirdly, things had started to improve recently. Was that because of you?" asked Tim. "They have all gone worse again now, though. My mum and mad are splitting up, and Bladen blames me."

"I know," said Larry Love-Who-You-Are.

"How do you know?" asked Tim confused.

"Oh, there is a lot that I know. That is my job, to see everything that is going on, to help the people involved understand it and then to support them through doing things differently. So far, your mum and dad have had some secret input, as has Bladen. In fact, I met her earlier today as she needed some guidance on who to pick for the job, and you were busy," replied Larry Love-Who-You-Are.

"Right, so am I the last to get some help?" asked Tim feeling slightly hurt that he must be the least important.

"No, actually you and Bladen were first. Can you remember this morning when you felt that you understood how clearly Bladen was feeling about herself? That was me. I swapped thought bubbles, and you saw Bladen's inner thoughts about herself and she saw yours. Mum got some of the thoughts too which was part of the plan. That was how it all began," continued Larry Love-Who-You-Are.

Tim felt relieved. He was glad that he hadn't been left until the end.

"Now, remind yourself of some of Bladen's inner thoughts. What she said earlier wasn't because she was being nasty or mean, it was actually because she was feeling hurt, scared and weak. When we feel low about ourselves, it is easier to blame others," justified Larry Love-Who-You-Are.

Tim suddenly remembered all of the times when he had done that in the past. In fact, just before Larry Love-Who-You-Are had arrived he was blaming Bladen for him not being able to go downstairs. "Yes, maybe you are right. But if I make it easy for Bladen, then she gets off with it too easily," muttered Tim a bit embarrassed at what he had just heard come out of his mouth.

"Who told you that?" challenged Larry Love-Who-You-Are. "Is it about winning and losing or is it about what is right and wrong? You say that Bladen would get away with it, but would she? Isn't she already going through enough? And she has said sorry, Tim. More importantly, you get the chance to move on with your feelings. Not forgiving Bladen keeps you stuck where you are right now. That sounds like you both lose, so what is the point of that?"

"But I am used to doing it this way. I don't know how to change it that quickly," explained Tim.

"Try it as a mini experiment now. See if it makes any difference. If you don't do anything differently Tim, nothing will change," said Larry Love-Who-You-Are.

"That is tough. I feel like I would be a fake because I don't really feel it," said Tim.

"Sometimes Tim, we all have to pretend we feel different in situations, in order to help us move through them and become more confident. Miss Hallatt in your school always dreads having to read messages out in assembly, so she fakes confidence in order to do what needs to be done. Is she a fake or is she doing what needs to be done?" asked Larry Love-Who-

You-Are.

"She's doing what needs to be done. I need to do what needs to be done. I will try and do this with Bladen now," said Tim.

Just as he opened the door, Bladen was coming out of the bathroom and gave him a half smile. Mum was also shouting from the kitchen that the bagels were ready.

"Come on, let's do this together. We need each other more than ever with all of this. No-one is going to understand how this feels better than us. I tell you one thing I do feel, though, is starving! Race you to the kitchen!" chirped Tim heading down the stairs at lightning speed.

Bladen followed with a gasp. Larry Love-Who-You-Are lay down for a minute on Tim's rumpled duvet. How wonderful this family were. All of them had worked really hard today and showed the flexibility that was needed to bring about positive change. He was sure that the family meeting together would be okay and if not,

he felt confident that the bagels could only
help to make this whole thing better!

Chapter 12

The weekend

Over the next few days, things in the O'Brien household felt more manageable. Things were still difficult and Mum and Dad were still living separately, but the family talk had helped Bladen and Tim understand things a little bit better. More importantly, they were beginning to realise that Mum and Dad splitting up wasn't because of them.

Mum had explained how people never stop growing and changing no matter how old they are, and that she and Dad had changed quite a lot over the last few years and didn't fit together as well as before. They wanted different things from their future to make them happy. The one thing that was not going to change, however, was that they would always and forever be Bladen and Tim's mum and dad who were, in fact, the most important thing on both their lists to make them the happiest.

At one point, Bladen had asked if it was possible for them to change more and like each other again in the future. Although Mum and Dad laughed, it was filled with an awkwardness that told the twins more than any words could have explained. However, Bladen and Tim both agreed afterwards that seeing Mum and Dad together and not arguing was better than how things had been for the many months, if not years, before.

Nevertheless, the first weekend that Bladen and Tim had to spend the weekend away from Mum at Dad's was tough. They had to pack, which was weird. Bladen and Tim went away on only one holiday a year, and Mum usually did the packing. This was different. Mum had not only specifically asked them to pack clothes, but also things that they might like to leave at Grandma and Grandad's for the next time they went.

Leaving their bedrooms was hard. Leaving the house was harder. But leaving Mum on her own for the weekend proved to be the hardest challenge of all. Both Bladen and Tim felt like they were splitting up from her. Millions of thoughts were filtering through their minds. What if Mum was lonely? What if she became ill? Who would look after her? What if she was sad and spent all weekend crying?

Mum did her best to reassure the twins, but she couldn't fake it completely. She was sad. She was terrified of feeling lonely in her own home. Luckily, she had thought that this might happen so had planned lots of lovely things with her friends. Being busy would hopefully reduce her missing the twins so much and more so, missing her old family life.

"Right, come on you two, we need to

get a move on. Otherwise, I will be late for lunch with the girls. Tim, have you got Dogger? Bladen, have you got Ratty?" shouted Mum.

"Yes," the twins chorused. Dogger and Ratty were essential weekend kit. There was no way that they would head off into this new stage without them. Dogger was a floppy pup that Tim had received from his Aunty Tracy when he was newly born. He had slept with Tim every night from the day he was old enough to claim him as his favourite toy.

Ratty had once been a plump, grey rodent but over the years had become a bit slender due to excess cuddling. In fact, Bladen had owned several Ratties over the years due to being lost or damaged. There had been many missions to the nearest Ratty store to make sure that she could sleep okay at night!

Bladen and Tim thudded their suitcases down the stairs. As they got to the front door, Mum came out of the kitchen. She had put on some make-up, but it had slightly been washed away with tears.

Mum went into her familiar Sergeant Major role which she did just before holidays each year. "Clothes?"

"Check," shouted Bladen and Tim.

"Pants and socks?"

"Check."

"Pyjamas?"

Tim quickly ran upstairs and returned with his PJs scrunched in his hand.

"Check," echoed the twins.

"Reading books?"

"Check."

"Homework?"

Bladen and Tim quickly dived into the cupboard under the stairs, pulled out their school rucksacks and removed their spelling logs and homework sheets.

"Check."

"Right, let's do this," said Mum pulling the twins into her with an enormous cuddle.

Their heavy cases were dragged to the car with heavy hearts. On the journey to see Dad, hardly anything was said. Tim was trying so hard not to cry. Bladen was using all her strength to not shout out at the top of her voice: 'Stop I don't want to do this, I can't do this."

The journey normally only seemed like five minutes, but this time it felt like hours. As they pulled up outside Grandma and Grandad's house, the front door was slightly ajar. "Go on then, you two. It looks like Dad is waiting for you already. Be good. Dad is dropping you back home on Sunday afternoon. Try not to spoil this with your arguing please and if I hear that you have argued, then there will be no screens for the rest of Sunday. Do you understand?" said Mum firmly.

"Yes Mum," replied Bladen and Tim.

Just then Dad opened the back door of the car. "Hey you two, are you ready to paaarrrttttyyyyy?"

This instantly annoyed Mum. She had to do all the serious stuff during the week like washing, ironing, shopping, organising and Dad got fun time. Although she bit her lip, her cheeks had coloured up and her forehead had sunk into a frown. The twins leant towards Mum to give her a kiss and then left the car.

"Mum, did you get me a present for Maggie's birthday party tomorrow?" asked Bladen popping her head into the opened front passenger window.

"Reo, you need to get a present and card before Bladen goes to the party tomorrow. I have been too busy this week doing everything else. So you can do that please because this weekend is my time to '*paaaarrrtttyyy*' too. See you kids, love you loads," snapped Mum and pulled out quickly from the roadside. A car slammed on its brakes and beeped its horn in fury at Mum not noticing it was there.

"See this is what you always do. Act without thinking. You nearly had an accident there. Yeah and thanks for not getting the present and card. Other things were more important, were they?" said Dad sarcastically.

Grandad came out of the front door and shouted the twins inside. "Can we stop all of this shouting, Reo? It isn't good for the children or anyone else to have to hear."

By this point, Mum had parked the car up and was now shouting back at Dad. "Do you have any idea how hard this week has been for me? Do you? I really don't need you criticising me as well," and with that, she slammed the door and drove off more carefully this time.

As Dad entered the house, Bladen and Tim were sitting very formally on Grandma and Grandad's sofa. This certainly didn't feel like home and although things had changed in lots of ways, Mum and Dad had very quickly gone back to their same old ways. Dad was also now in a mood.

"Right well, I had lots of things planned for this weekend, but now we will have to go shopping for this present. Do you have to go to this party Bladen?" ranted Dad.

"Yes, I would really like to. It is Maggie's, and we are becoming good friends. Please Dad, please let me go," pleaded Bladen.

Dad suddenly remembered the dream he had the other day that showed him how little the twins think of themselves sometimes. He was pricked with guilt again about all the times he had been harsh on the twins or the many times he had placed unhelpful orders on them.

"Sorry Bladen, of course you can go to the party. I am just a bit cross at your mum at the moment. Let's have tea and then we can go and get it tonight before the shops close. We aren't going to let this spoil our weekend, are we?" asked Dad with his arms open wide, welcoming the twins in for a big bear hug.

Although the weekend didn't begin well, all in all, it turned out to be okay. Grandma and Grandad made an extra effort to make the weekend special. Bladen enjoyed Maggie's party. Tim and Dad had some quality time playing football in the park. Mum phoned several times to see how the twins were and shared reassuring stories that she was having a lovely weekend too. Dogger and Ratty made different sleeping arrangements familiar. Bladen and Tim shared their difficult feelings with each other.

"Do you think we will be doing this forever?" asked Tim as they were going to sleep, after having been allowed to stay up a bit later to watch the results of the Saturday night talent show.

"I don't know. I can't imagine Dad living here all the time. If they don't get back together maybe he will get somewhere else to live," said Bladen.

Tim spent many minutes thinking about what the future might be like. "I don't like us all not being together, I have this very sad feeling in my tummy. I feel bad about all the naughty things I have done in the past. I wish I had been a perfect son," whispered Tim.

Bladen didn't reply. Instead, a soft, heavy breathing sound could be heard escaping her mouth as she drifted into light sleep.

Larry Love-Who-You-Are heard, though. "Hey, you. Don't be so harsh on yourself. You are who you are, Tim. You might not be perfect, but I don't know anyone who is. Remember it is not about the best, it is about good enough. If you spend too much time criticising yourself, you will make yourself feel worse. You need to start seeing yourself as good enough Tim, even with your faults."

"But maybe if I was kinder or cleverer or better behaved, none of this would have happened," said Tim.

"We are all changing all the time. This experience is changing you. It is making you learn and grow as a person. I am not saying that we shouldn't change, it is just that we need to do it with self-love rather than self-hate," declared Larry Love-Who-You-Are.

Tim's thoughts began to merge with sleep. Before he had a chance to reply, he too was heading into dreamland where he could mull over all the things that he was learning about himself.

Larry Love-Who-You-Are tucked Ratty and Dogger into the arms of Bladen and Tim. They were good kids. Things were moving steadily in the right direction and with more understanding, effort and time he knew they would realise it too.

Chapter 13

Trials

The months that followed offered many challenges to Bladen and Tim in many different areas. Some of the tasks included:

Personal

- being kinder about who they are

- recognising their good points and accepting their faults

- keeping things in perspective when things go wrong

- reminding themselves regularly of things they do that make them proud. If they can't think of anything for several days, do something that does

- being braver, in being honest and

sharing opinions

- trying to take more responsibility for their role in their life

- being their own best friend

Relationships

- being honest and respectful towards people

- recognising they are worthy of respect

- noticing that other people do consider their feelings and views

- making more effort with relationships and friendships

- trying not to blame themselves for the stresses of the trial separation between Mum and Dad

Home

- stopping and thinking before reacting negatively so as not to feel worse about themselves afterwards

- remembering how sensitive each other is and not always seeing negative behaviour as meanness (though sometimes kids are kids!)

School

- trying to be more confident even when they didn't feel it

- attempting new things rather than not trying at all

- taking on new challenges and seeing what they could cope with

None of these challenges came easy, well not at first anyway. However, one thing they did notice was that the more often they faced these problems head on, the easier they became. The hardest part of the whole process was doing something for the first time. Bladen was once asked to speak in an assembly. Obviously, her first reaction was to find as many reasons as possible why not to do it. But things were changing now.

Since she had met Larry Love-Who-You-Are, she noticed that she didn't always go for the easiest option. In the past when things seemed difficult, Bladen usually stopped which meant she was left beaten by the problem and nothing good was achieved. Now she found herself trying harder! So although the assembly offer was hard and she even made a simple mistake, it appeared to go unnoticed and she got a round of applause from all the teachers and then the children. This was due to her thoughts over time slowly beginning to see the possibilities. Better still the more new experiences she tried, the better she felt about herself and newer labels were created for others to see who she was.

As Bladen saw herself as happier, so did other people and they wanted to be around her happiness. The harder she worked on school challenges, the cleverer she looked, and classmates asked her to help them with their work. The more confident she pretended she was, the more special jobs and responsibility she got which made her feel valued and important. It was a *win win win win win win win win win* situation!!!

Tim noticed the same. Every year he had gone for the football trials in school, but always did it because it was what the boys did and if he didn't do it, there would be no boys in the playground at lunchtime and he certainly didn't want that! Never had Tim approached the trials with hope. He was playing football more regularly now, not just at school but with Dad. Last time they had a kick around in the park, Tim saved four out of five penalties against Dad, and that was without gloves. Seeing Tim's potential talent, Dad had taken Tim straight down to the local sports shop and bought some top quality goalie gloves. It was now a regular part of the time spent with Dad, and this had boosted Tim's self-confidence in many ways.

The football trials this year felt different

for Tim. In reality, they were no different to the previous eight that Mr White had organised. The difference was in Tim's head. Because Tim was being more honest about his feelings now, Bladen knew how important this trial was to Tim and so, she managed to talk Maggie and a few of the others into going up to the field to show their support for Tim and watch him.

In the changing room, Tim was suddenly faced with the reality of what he was going to do. All the boys were giddily getting ready putting on their football boots and talking about who was a good player and was likely to get in. Obviously, no one mentioned Tim. He looked at his goalie gloves. He looked at his boots. Something was stopping him even putting them on. He was so close to not even trying. Why should he? This would be his third rejection. Maybe he was fooling himself.

As he looked at his football boots, the laces began to open wider. Larry Love-Who-You-Are was slowly loosening them so that his feet could slip in more easily.

"Do you know what the hardest part of this football trial is?" he asked.

"Yes I do, only too well. Messing up, not being picked...again, and looking like an idiot. How many do you want?" answered Tim feeling weak and worried.

"Nope," began Larry Love-Who-You-Are. "Putting on your football boots."

"No way," whispered Tim. "That is the easy bit. It is all the other stuff that makes it difficult."

"If you don't put on your boots Tim, you will not achieve any of the possibilities. It takes more courage to put your boots on when you are filled with dread and self-doubt than anything else. Once they are on, you are committed to trying and then the possibilities might happen. You are more likely to regret what you don't do than what you do," explained Larry Love-Who-You-Are.

Tim looked at the boots, then at the gloves and finally at Larry Love-Who-You-Are. What he said seemed to make sense, but it would be so much easier to hide away from the awfulness that could lie ahead.

He slipped his left foot into his football boot. Should he do this? Could he do this? Larry Love-Who-You-Are beamed a proud smile. Tim tightened up the laces. Just as he thought he couldn't do up the next boot, Robbie came and plonked himself

on the bench beside him. Larry Love-Who-You-Are quickly hid inside the other boot.

"Are you going for Goalkeeper, Tim? Me and the boys think you could do it this year. That goal you saved last week was mega, you are a legend. I'd definitely want you on my team. Good luck. See you out there."

Larry Love-Who-You-Are gave an agreeing nod whilst escaping from inside the dark, slightly smelly boot.

This was just what Tim needed to hear. This perked up his inner confidence. Maybe he could do it. He spent a moment thinking about what the worst was that could happen. The worst thing would be that he got told no...again. However, he had survived that before so he could do it again. He quickly put on his other footy boot and his gloves. Larry Love-Who-You-Are was right, now they were on there was no going back and he was committed to giving it a go.

Out on the field, all the boys were warming up. Mr White always began with some football exercises, dribbling around a set of cones, 30 seconds of 'keepy-uppies', some five-a-side games and then finishing with a penalty shootout. Bladen and the girls had perched themselves on the edge of the pitch, and other spectators were starting to join them.

Tim stood with the other boys in his year group looking at Mr White, but not hearing a word that was coming out of his mouth. His thoughts were hi-jacked with negative thinking about himself. What he missed was that he was going to mix up the whole team this year and play people in different places. Robbie gave him a nudge, but Tim thought it was because he hadn't been listening. He brought himself to the present by breathing heavily in through his nose and out through his mouth.

The trials began. Tim messed up completely in the dribbling, but that had never been a strength. However, he managed to pull it back with the keepy-uppies and he came third on that. All that practice with Dad had paid off. During the matches, Tim thought he played okay. He had one game in goal and one game where he played outfield. Although he never scored any goals, he did manage to save two when he was in goal, which got great cheers from the crowd.

The final test was the penalty shootout. Mr White asked if anyone was interested in playing in goal. Only one person put their hand up, Marshal, who had been a goalie in Year 4.

"Tim will he is brilliant in goal," shouted Robbie.

Tim looked shocked. Marshal looked annoyed. Mr White looked pleased. Bladen and Larry Love-Who-You-Are looked ecstatic. They knew that Tim might have stayed safe if he could.

"Right, I have 14 players who have

stood out today. We will do the first seven shooting penalties against Marshal and the second seven against Tim. Marshal, come and get into position please," ordered Mr White.

"Can I borrow your goalie gloves, Tim? I forgot mine," asked Marshal desperately.

Tim was flooded with choices. The gloves might give him the advantage he needed. However, he wasn't going to win anyway so he might as well do something nice instead he thought. He removed the gloves and passed them to Marshal.

"Cheers mate," shouted Marshal striding over to his goalie position.

The seven players were placed into shootout penalty order. Marshal managed to save five out of the seven goals. Marshal was pleased and nodded confidently towards Tim, and handed over the gloves.

Tim walked the long walk into goal while tightening up his gloves. The gloves felt firm, secure. Oh, how he wished that he felt the same. Then for the first time ever, he heard himself say something positive.

"Come on Tim, give it your best shot. Penalties are your thing. You can do this."

The first player got into position. SAVE. A cheer erupted from Bladen and the ever increasing crowd. Even Shan, the saddest girl in the whole school, had come to see what all the fuss was about.

The second player kicked. SAVE. Tim looked round as he thought he had done a home goal that time. A bigger applause erupted.

The third player paced up and down and launched the ball. MISS. Everyone but Marshal sighed. Tim's confidence sank.

Player four thrust the ball at the goal's top right corner. It skimmed Tim's fingers. Another MISS.

Player five was ready. Tim needed to save the next three penalties to draw.

SAVE. The crowd went crazy.

Player six was in position. A left footer. SAVE. Tim had pulled it back. Mr White was now watching behind his hands.

Player seven. Tim had to save this one to be in with a chance. The ball was kicked. Tim couldn't decide left or right. He threw himself as high as he could to the left and the ball hit the bottom right corner. MISS. Everyone chorused "Noooooooooooooooooo."

Tim was gutted. It was all over. Another rejection, another failure moment. He headed towards his friends with his head low. Robbie rushed to his side. "You were awesome, Tim. Okay, Marshal saved more penalties, but you put so much effort into it. I would pick you."

Tim half smiled. Robbie was becoming a really good friend.

"Well done boys, you have all played brilliantly. I have a lot to think about now, but I will have the final team chosen by tomorrow lunchtime, same place and time as today.

Bladen rushed over to Tim. "Well done for giving it your best shot Tim, you played brilliantly. All the girls thought you were ace."

"Thanks Bladen, but I still won't get picked so it was all a waste of time. I should never have tried for it anyway. It is just another rejection," replied Tim feeling very low.

"You don't know that for sure," said Bladen.

"I DO BLADEN. I DO. NOW GO AWAY AND LEAVE ME ALONE." He hated himself even more now for what he had just said and done.

The next 23 hours were going to be tough for Tim, and everyone else, thought Bladen as she headed towards her friends and feeling helpless.

Chapter 14

Fear

On the way home from school, Tim hardly said a word. Bladen tried several times to start a conversation, but nothing worked. Tim was locked away inside and Bladen knew only too well that when this happened, it was not easy to get out of. Bladen reminded herself of times when she felt like this. The sense of failure was enormous. The sensation of dread was huge. The world felt dark and cold and lonely.

When they arrived home, Tim dropped his bag, kicked off his shoes and headed straight upstairs to his room. Mum came out of the living room. "Hey you two, have you had a good day?" asked Mum.

"Okay...ish," replied Bladen, hoping

Mum wouldn't ask any more about it.

"Are you okay, Tim?" shouted Mum up the stairs and in the direction of Tim's bedroom. Although Tim had heard her, he couldn't even fake a response so decided to not say anything at all.

"I think he just wants some time on his own," explained Bladen.

"Oh, alright. I will make you both a snack. Toasted teacakes and fruit on its way," said Mum heading towards the kitchen.

Bladen headed upstairs. As she was about to go into her room, she decided that she would just check one more time if Tim was okay. She knocked gently on his door. "Tim, can I come in?" No response. "Please don't feel like you are on your own with this. That will just make you feel worse. You can talk to me anytime. I just wanted you to know that."

Tim never moved. His eyes were staring

at the point on the ceiling where the jelly alien was still hanging after being thrown there roughly 18 months ago. Tim's mind was flooded with thoughts. How could he ever show his face in school again? Why had he gone for the football trials again? Weren't two rejections enough? He must be stupid to put himself through that again. No way could he go to the lunchtime meeting. How could he face everyone tomorrow after the team had been selected? Everyone would know what he knew only too well...he was pathetic at everything.

Larry Love-Who-You-Are recognised that enough was enough and Tim needed to be snapped out of the negative groove his mind had slipped into. "Hi Tim, looks like you need a friend at the moment."

Tim rolled onto his side and scrunched himself up into a tight ball.

"Listen. You are getting today out of perspective. You are letting your imagination run wild, and it is creating lots of situations that are just guesses. Your brain is trying to predict the future without the facts. This is called fortune telling, and every brain does it sometimes. It is our way of trying to find answers to problems, but it is rarely helpful and rarely true," clarified Larry Love-Who-You-Are.

"I messed up today. I showed myself up in front of everyone. I am rubbish at everything, and everyone knows it. What isn't fact about that?" whispered Tim weakly.

"You are blinkering out all the good things that you did today. You showed real courage by even going for it. You were kind to Marshal, who needed your gloves. You played better than at any of your last trials because you are a better player now," explained Larry Love-Who-You-Are, trying hard to activate Tim's positivity.

"No way can I go to the meeting

tomorrow. In fact, I don't even think that I can face going to school. I might make myself sick and then I can stay off and hide away from it until it calms down a bit," said Tim.

"Okay, so let's imagine that's what you do. What are the positives of you avoiding school tomorrow?" asked Larry Love-Who-You-Are.

"Erm, that's easy. I won't have to hear the results that I am not in the team. I won't have to watch everyone looking at me thinking I have failed. I won't have to spend another day wearing the label 'failure'," replied Tim.

"Okay, so what would be the negatives of you not going into school tomorrow?" continued Larry Love-Who-You-Are.

"There are no negatives," responded Tim far too quickly.

"Think again, Tim. What would be the costs to your life if you didn't go to school tomorrow?" recapped Larry Love-Who-You-Are.

"Well, I would miss a day of learning, I suppose," muttered Tim.

"And?" prompted Larry Love-Who-You-Are.

"And people might think I have skived off school which won't make me look too good. Then I might get told off. Also, they might think I am weak, which I am anyway," began Tim.

"What will you think of yourself?" asked Larry Love-Who-You-Are.

"I will be reminded that I am a wimp. I will feel bad that I have lied. I will not like who I am," mumbled Tim, not liking what he heard himself saying one bit.

"We can all feel those things Tim, but you have a choice. Do you want to be a slave to those feelings and give in to them or do you want to challenge them and be better? Everyone feels scared in difficult situations, but courage and personal strength comes right out of **FEAR** – **F**ace **E**verything **A**nd **R**ecover," explained Larry Love-Who-You-Are. "None of us know what we can do until we try it. If we always stay safe and hide from tricky things, we never grow as a person. We stay stuck and unhappy."

"But no way could I face going into the meeting tomorrow. I just couldn't do it," whimpered Tim wiping tears from his eyes.

"Okay, so what is the worse that could happen if you went in?" asked Larry Love-Who-You-Are.

"Easy. They tell me I'm not on the team, and then everybody laughs at me and calls me a a a...loser," sniffled Tim.

"Did that happen last time you weren't picked?" questioned Larry Love-Who-You-Are.

"Well, no but I always expected it too," answered Tim.

"Ahh, that was your fortune telling again. However, you weren't right were you? See, your brain isn't always your friend with what it guesses. Also, I am not sure Mr White would allow that to happen, would he?" continued Larry Love-Who-You-Are.

"I just can't do it. I can't go and hear that I'm not in again," said Tim beginning to cry again.

"We need to get you ready to face your FEAR. So get comfortable and close your eyes. Now, imagine that you are watching yourself on television thinking about heading towards the field. How does that feel?" began Larry Love-Who-You-Are.

"Awful. I can tell that I am scared. I don't want to do it," said Tim.

"Okay. What is your imagined fear of joining them, with zero being the least and10 being the most? asked Larry Love-Who-You-Are.

"About a seven," pondered Tim.

"In reality, what level of fear do you think joining them would be?" continued Larry Love-Who-You-Are.

"Well, there isn't any really dangerous things, so walking over would maybe probably really be a two," replied Tim.

"Good. Good. Can you see why we are doing this, Tim? Now I want you to imagine yourself walking over to the football meeting. This will be more uncomfortable, but it is important," explained Larry Love-Who-You-Are.

"Yes, this feels more difficult. I feel nervous and want to run towards the classroom."

"Keep doing it. Walk towards Mr White. Now, imagine everyone is smiling at you as you arrive and Mr White is patting you on the shoulder reassuringly as you get there. How does that feel?" asked Larry Love-Who-You-Are.

"That feels good. I don't feel as anxious. I feel stronger, braver."

"Brilliant. Now lock that feeling inside of you. You created those feelings of strength and courage. They are always inside of you, but sometimes you just need to find them. Winners never give up and when they lose, they try harder. Do you feel that you could go to the meeting tomorrow?" asked Larry Love-Who-You-Are hopeful.

"Well, I am still dreading it but I know I have to do it if I want to recover from these horrible feelings of worthlessness. I would rather be a brave failure than a weak one," answered Tim with a flicker of power in his belly.

Larry Love-Who-You-Are held out his hand for a 'well-done' high five. They both giggled, although Tim did so with slightly too much force and sent Larry Love-Who-You-Are tumbling backwards through the air until he landed upside down at the edge of the bed!

"Thank you, Larry Love-Who-You-Are. I will face the meeting tomorrow. I have done it before and I will do it again." Tim nodded with a sense of purpose.

"Well done Tim, I am proud of you. You will need to work hard this evening not to let the fear kick back in. Hold tightly onto those special values that you have – strength and determination. I will be watching out for you tomorrow," explained Larry Love-Who-You-Are and with that, he tiptoed out of the opened window.

Tim spent a couple of minutes reminding himself what had just happened, while locking the positive

feelings deep inside so that he could
draw on them whenever he needed them.
Tomorrow was going to be a big test but
one that he wanted desperately to pass.

Chapter 15

Becoming a winner

When Tim woke up the next morning, he felt sick. Not tummy bug sick, but nervous sick. He also felt sad. He had done everything Larry Love-Who-You-Are had suggested he do in order to keep the positive feelings alive, but they had sadly diluted overnight, and now only a trickle remained. He pulled himself out of bed, even though staying there for the day seemed like a good option.

He remembered some of the things that Larry Love-Who-You-Are had told him over the last few months. *'The hardest part of doing the football trials is putting your football boots on.'* Yes, the hardest part of getting to school was definitely getting out of bed just then. *Just because something is difficult doesn't mean that you stop trying –*

you need to try harder. Today was going to be very difficult indeed, but he was going to face it and recover.

Tim went downstairs for breakfast. Mum was in a rush getting things ready for work and adding ingredients to the slow cooker, as it was her late night at work tonight. "Don't forget, you two, that you need to go to your dad's tonight after school. Dad knows about it. Then he is going to drop you off here afterwards. We will eat then. Did you hear me, Tim? You seem a bit distracted."

Tim looked up from the cereal he was stirring and not eating. "Yes, fine Mum. We go to Dad's and eat when we get back."

"Are you okay, Tim?" asked Bladen.

"Yes. No. I don't know. It is the trial results today. I really, really don't want to know that I have messed up again. I wish I could just hide until it is all over and everyone has forgotten how I failed again," started Tim.

"You played well, Tim. Best I have ever seen you. Everyone who was watching wanted you to win," explained Bladen.

"Oh, don't tell me that. It is hard enough knowing I have let the boys down, but not the crowd as well," he said dropping his head. The drop in his neck activated his determination. A surge of positive power travelled from his mind to his body. He sat up with a fierce stance. "But I am going to face the reality today, with strength not with weakness."

Larry Love-Who-You-Are clapped with joy. While Tim had been sleeping, he had re-wired parts of Tim's brain and body. Any negative body language, like drooping shoulders or a frowning forehead, would activate the opposite response. It was good to see it having a positive effect.

"Great, Tim. That is a superb attitude. You have changed so much from how you were a few months ago and to how you were last night. I think at last you and I are happier with life, don't you?" asked Bladen with interest.

"Yes, I suppose so. I still feel scared sometimes though and still don't think I am good enough, but I know what to do about it now, and that really helps to make things better. You are loads different too. It is good to see you happier, and I don't feel like we are in competition with each other anymore. It feels like we are on the same side again, like we used to be," said Tim.

Bladen smiled. Tim was right. They not only stuck up for themselves now, but they also stuck up for each other. They had learned so much.

"Right, come on you two, shoes on. We need to be out now. Do you want me to drop you both off on my way to work?" asked Mum.

"Yes please," chorused Bladen and Tim grabbing bags and heading for the car.

When they arrived at school, there were only a few other children in the playground. As Bladen and Tim decided to head up towards their usual spot, Mr White was coming out of the PE hall. "I'll see you at the football meeting later, Tim. Don't forget."

How could he forget? This semi-frown triggered more courage and determination. "Of course, Sir," said Tim surprising himself at his confidence. He knew today was going to go very slow and just wished he could get this bit over with and then move on.

"Yes, I can imagine that. Well, at least we have a good morning planned. We are finishing our coding for the computer games this morning, then we all get a chance to play in each other's games and evaluate them," enthused Bladen.

"Yes, I suppose," said Tim with a sigh. Before he knew it, a mighty wave of bravery rippled through his body which he felt he had to use. "Race you to the trees."

"You're on," shouted Bladen, and they both sprinted with all their might to the top of the field. Once there, they flopped onto the grass and lay panting, looking up at the morning sky.

Tim felt brilliant. He had never felt so strong. The answer to the trials didn't seem as important anymore. He felt like he had won something far greater. He had won a better him. He had won stage one of positive self-belief. This was worth more than any football position as this could last forever if he looked after it. He smiled a true smile, just as the bell went for registration.

"Come on," said Tim. "Let's do this."

The morning actually went quite quickly for Tim. Maybe it was because the urgency for the football meeting had been removed. He surprised himself by feeling calm. As the class piled into the cloakroom, Robbie gave Tim a friendly shoulder barge. "Who do you think is in then?"

"Well, it won't be me," laughed Tim.

"Hey, you never know! You played well. Shame about that last penalty, though. Come on, let's go and see," said Robbie.

Tim gulped. "Yes, let's see."

As the boys gathered together, the air was filled with excitement and tension. Tim was watching. Some boys were

jogging on the spot to look professional. Others were lying on the grass without a care in the world. Robbie and a few of the other lads were kicking a pretend football around. It eventually came towards Tim, and he dived to save it which made the boys cheer and run over to him, rubbing his hair and hugging him like they had just won the FA cup final!

Eventually, Mr White could be seen heading over to the field, and the boys all stopped. Suddenly this felt serious.

"Right lads, thank you for attending today. This has been a really tough 24 hours for me. There was some brilliant football played yesterday and some great skill. I was also impressed by the general attitude of you as potential players. So after lots of thinking, I have finalised the squad that I would like to play for the match with Croft House Primary School this season. Those who are not in, try not to be too disappointed. It was a very high standard this year and with a bit more practice there is no reason why you couldn't be selected here next year or in your new school," explained Mr White.

Oh well, thought Tim. If he was going to lose, it was good to know that he was losing to a high standard rather than a low one.

"So the 12 selected boys are – Mason Bell, Callum Dixon, Braiden Hones, Marshal Smith, Logan Biggs, Ramarni Robson, Chris Edwards, Caine Peterson, Humza Parwaiz, Mitchel Woods, Robbie Tucker and..."

Tim listened to every name, but listening now was proving difficult, although he liked this state of hope. Once the last name was read out, the hope might go.

"And Tim O'Brien," shouted Mr White in Tim's direction.

Was Tim hearing things? Had he just been selected or told off for not listening? He looked at the group of boys. Robbie, Ramarni and Mason were all looking at him with excited grins and thumbs up.

Oh my goodness, he was in! He had been selected!

"I would just like to spend a minute talking about how impressed I was with Tim O'Brien yesterday. Throughout the trials Tim was very nervous, I think anyone watching would have noticed that, but he kept going. He also showed great team spirit with other players when they needed him which are two of the qualities that I want in my football team. I know Tim has trialled many times, but this is a lesson to you all. No matter how far you are away from your goal, you'll never know what you could achieve until you try," said Mr White.

Tim was in shock. The words Mr White had just spoken could have come out of Larry Love-Who-You-Are's mouth. Had Mr White experienced some Blink magic too? Bladen ran over to Tim and hugged him. "Get off," he said. "I am on the football team now, too cool to be seen with my sister!" laughed Tim.

"You did it. You are on the team, and you got a special mention. I am so proud of you, Tim. All your hard work has paid off. Well done," said Bladen.

His new teammates surrounded him. He was part of something he had yearned for for several years. He couldn't help but wonder what today would have felt like if he hadn't attended and if he had stayed in bed all day. Determination and courage had become his new best friends and with them by his side, Tim's fear of his future abilities was beginning to change from doubt to excitement. What a day. What a brilliant day.

"Ditto," echoed Larry Love-Who-You-Are from up in a nearby tree. He was beaming with pride, not just at Tim's achievements with the football, but how both he and Bladen had worked so hard at changing their inner message about who and what they are. A period of celebration was just around the corner for all.

Chapter 16

You are what you believe you are

One thing that surprised both Bladen and Tim was how long these waves of good feelings lasted these days. Usually, when good things happened, like getting some new football trainers or doing well on a spelling test, the positive feeling faded very quickly. The big difference now was that these good feelings were stored somewhere special within themselves, whereas in the past good feelings came from situations or things outside of them. Nevertheless, now that their positivity radars had been activated internally, they noticed that other things began to feel better too.

Bladen noticed that she felt genuinely happy for Tim. Not threatened. Not jealous. Happy and proud. Tim noticed this too and gave her patience and gratitude in return. They also noticed that Mum and Dad seemed to be more positive, not just with them but with each other. Although Dad still reacted quickly at times and forgot to think before he spoke, Bladen and Tim felt like they could buffer these comments rather than them hurt them so much. Mum was most noticeably different. She seemed to have more time to spare. In reality, she didn't at all, but she prioritised the twins' needs and recognised the importance of listening to them.

They also felt like Mum and Dad were kinder to each other. Dad even stayed for tea more often. Although they were still separated, Bladen and Tim had accepted that they were both happier people now. Of course, Bladen and Tim secretly hoped that their family would one day be a complete unit again but on the whole, things were the best they had been for a long time. That felt good enough, so anything extra would be a bonus.

One rainy afternoon, Bladen was sorting out her wardrobe in her bedroom and came across an old diary. As she opened it she was saddened by what she read. Seven-year-old Bladen was so negative about herself and about her life. She doodled dark, unhappy pictures. She had listed many things that she was rubbish at. She also listed even more things about what she hated about Tim!

She went next door to show Tim. "Look what I have found. It is my old diary from

when I was in Y3. I was so unhappy about myself. I was even more unhappy about you! I listed 18 things as to why you were annoying!" laughed Bladen.

"Ha ha, I think I did that once about you, but I had 24!" joked Tim. "How many of those things do you still feel about yourself now?"

"A few. But not half as many. I am still not very good at French. I might always get cross quicker than I would like and I still bite my nails when I am worried," said Bladen working down the list.

"Yes, but we all have faults. No-one is perfect. There are loads of things I still don't love about me but they are part of me, and luckily I have found lots more strengths that I do like.

"Hey, let's make a list each now. First, let's write the things we like about each other and then what we like about ourselves," suggested Bladen excitedly.

"Okay," said Tim. "But we need to do this honestly so let's also write three flaws that each other has that make us happy to be imperfect."

"Yes, yes. I like it," clapped Bladen amazed at how motivated she was to face up to her weaknesses.

Ten minutes later the twins got back to each other and read out their lists. Bladen went first.

"So Tim, this is what makes you wonderfully imperfect. You:

1. are patient

2. are funny

3. are untidy

4. are brilliant at drawing

5. are an excellent goalie

6. have the smelliest feet in the world

7. are intelligent

8. don't give up

9. ratty when you are hungry."

Tim smiled. He liked that list and even though he could argue the smelly feet and rattiness points, he knew really that Bladen was right. "Thanks. This time last year I wouldn't have believed you if you had said those things about me, but now I have some evidence to say I am those things because I have pushed myself to experience them. Right, now your list, Bladen. You:

1. are kind

2. are caring

3. are supportive

4. are honest

5. take things too personally sometimes

6. have brilliant handwriting

7. get cross quickly

8. don't stay in a mood for long

9. are a fun sister

Bladen pretended to be in a mood and crossed her arms sulkily. "Get cross too quickly. What do you mean? I never get cross. I can't believe you said that," ranted Bladen and then fell on the bed laughing.

"This list is so different to how you seemed before," said Tim.

"Because it is. When I thought all negative things about myself, I *felt* negative things about myself, and that stopped me doing new stuff as I thought there was no point. I actually think I am alright now. Not perfect, but okay and I like that. Also, the more new things I try, the better I seem to get at it. So then I have more successes to remind myself of. What do you think has made you feel different about who you are, Tim?" asked Bladen.

"For me the biggest thing was finding

the courage to face difficult situations rather than running away from them. If all you do is hide, you never know what you can cope with or achieve. Something clicked in me one day, and I changed from an *'I can't'* person to an *'I can'* person and although not everything is possible, I now believe that if you think you can – you can!" explained Tim. "Should we do our own list now?"

"Yes great. Meet you back here in 10 minutes," replied Bladen.

Larry Love-Who-You-Are lay down on the bookshelf and smiled a deep content smile. Bladen and Tim had been developing positive self-esteem. They had learned how to see something better about themselves. They had changed their thoughts which had changed their feelings but more so, they had changed who and what they believed they were.

Tim scribbled away at his desk. His list now included:

- ✓ I have good friends who like me

- ✓ I work hard

- ✓ I will always try

- ✓ Getting things wrong doesn't make me a failure

- ✓ I am stronger than I thought

- ✓ I have confidence in myself

- ✓ I have things to be proud of

- ✓ I am not perfect, but I am okay

Bladen's list was very similar:

- ✓ I can handle negative things better

- ✓ I am more in control of who I want to be

- ✓ I can do it if I try

- ✓ I am not scared of getting things wrong anymore, I am learning

- ✓ I am a good friend

✓ My life is good

✓ I feel loved

✓ I like feeling like this

Tim and Bladen headed downstairs. Life felt good.

Mum had just finished making some popcorn and they were all going to get snuggled up on the sofa to watch a film together. There was just one more job that Larry Love-Who-You-Are needed to do before he headed off into his seven days of fun. He picked up Tim's pencil. One last thing needed to be added to both of their lists. He began writing.

You are what you believe...

Maybe you could finish it off!

The End

The Blinks Reference Manuals

Accompanying all the Blinks' novels are Reference Manuals for parents, carers, older siblings, teachers and professionals. The supportive booklets provide a greater understanding of the psychology of all emotions and how they can impact on other developmental issues. They also provide a lot of 'top tips' of what works best for children and young people whilst growing up and some activity questions that can be used as a starting point to initiate emotive dialogue or discussion.

Look out for The Blinks 4 – due for release in 2017.

For a full listing of all the books in the series go to – www.theblinks.co.uk

Acknowledgements

First, I would like to thank my daughter Lily for her commitment and dedication in proofreading to the highest standard and also for becoming Head of Despatch which, as with everything, she does so well. Other proofreading credits go to Auntie Karin and Janet you are both awesome. Thank you so much for your time and effort you are a brilliant team. Thank you also to Jill for your editing expertise.

My eternal thanks, as always, go to my wonderful illustrator, Rachel Pesterfield whose creative imagination and detail adds some welcomed colourful magic to the pages. Also to Grace for your brilliant model poses and Mum Julie for your patience. With thanks also to my publisher Gail, who is highly appreciated in getting these books out there and for her loyalty to their cause, promoting them whenever possible.

A special thank you to Hallam FM's Cash 4 Kids for sponsoring 'The Blinks' and hopefully getting copies to every primary school in South Yorkshire.

I would also like to say a heartfelt thank you to Evie Mae, who took the time to write me my very first fan letter. It currently has pride of place on my noticeboard and keeps me going on my more difficult writing days.

As always, none of this would be possible without the constant love and support of my family, friends and neighbours, especially from my lovely friend, Harry; you are a star and your excitement for 'The Blinks' warms my heart.

I would also like to recognise the wonderful people who have moved on from our lives this year. Some are people

I know personally, some are special to those I care about and some are creative legends. Please share a moment to remember Gareth, Linda, Julie F, Jo S, Victoria Wood, David Bowie, Prince and Mohammed Ali.

About the Author

Andrea Chatten- MSc, MBPsS,

PGCLandM, Bed (Hons), Dip.CBT

Andrea Chatten has been a specialised teacher for over 25 years; working with children from ages 5-16 with emotional and behavioural difficulties. She is currently the Director and Lead of Unravel CEBPC Ltd in and around Sheffield and across the UK.

Developing positive, trusting relationships has always been at the heart of her practice with children and young people in order to nudge them into improved psychological well-being.

Over the years, Andrea has developed and applied many positive developmental psychology approaches.

This insight is incorporated into her stories in order to help children, young people and their families to gain more of an understanding and potential strategies to try, in order to deal with a range of behavioural issues that children and young people could experience.

Andrea created 'The Blinks' so that parents and carers could also benefit from reading the books with their children, particularly if they identify with the children in the stories, and their own family circumstances. Both parent or carer and child could learn how to manage early forms of psychological distress as a natural part of growing up rather than it become problematic when not addressed in its early stages.

The Blinks is a series of books that discreetly apply lots of psychological theory throughout the story including Cognitive Behavioural Therapy, Developmental and Positive Psychology approaches.

www.unravelcebpc.co.uk

www.theblinks.co.uk

Facebook - /Theblinksbooks

Twitter - @BlinksThe

'The Blinks – Worry' is the first novel in the Blinks series of books.

The first book in the series is to help all children and young people understand how worry and anxiety present. It is written as a fiction book with many messages and guidance woven into the stories about Amanda and her friends.'

'The Blinks – Anger' is the second novel in
the Blinks series of books.

This book is to help all children and young
people understand the strong emotion of
anger and what to do with it to remain in
charge. Robbie's life has never been great,
but the events over the last few years have
slowly made him more and more unhappy
and angry. One day it all gets too much,
and his anger erupts!

TO ORDER A COPY OF EITHER OF THE FIRST TWO BOOKS IN THE SERIES GO TO – www.theblinks.co.uk

You can also purchase a printed copy of either book or the Kindle versions on AMAZON.

The next novel in the Blinks series is 'The Blinks – Sadness' and will be available in 2017.

If you wish to receive advanced notification of new releases and access to limited editions and more Blinks' news, then please sign up for free and become a FAN of Andrea Chatten's (author) at-

www.oodlebooks.com